KAREN BLUEJEANS

PATHWAY TO GLORY

GEORGE HORSE

ARCHWAY
PUBLISHING

Archway Publishing books may be ordered through booksellers or by contacting:

Archway Publishing
1663 Liberty Drive
Bloomington, IN 47403
www.archwaypublishing.com
844-669-3957

Scripture taken from the King James Version of the Bible.

ISBN: 978-1-6657-1251-4 (sc)
ISBN: 978-1-6657-1252-1 (e)

Library of Congress Control Number: 2021919432

Print information available on the last page.

Archway Publishing rev. date: 05/20/2022

Dedicated To:

Jessica Armstrong

1 – St. Lawrence River
2 – *Isle d'Orleans*
3 – *Pt Levy*
4 – Quebec City, Lower Town
5 – Quebec City, Upper Town
6 – *Beauport*
7 – Montmorency Falls
8 – St. Charles River
9 – *Ance au Foulon*
10 – Plain of Abraham
11 – St. Louis Gate
12 – Beaver Lodge
13 – *To Montreal*
14 – To *Above the Falls*
15 – Flagship, *Prince of Wales*

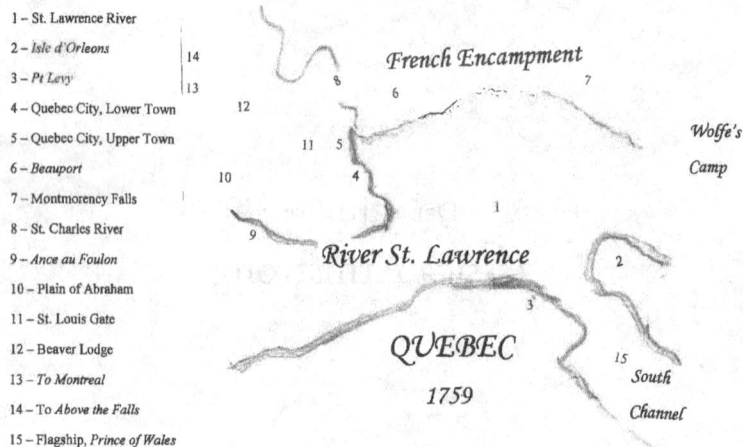

French Encampment

Wolfe's
Camp

River St. Lawrence

QUEBEC

1759

South
Channel

INTRODUCTION

Four F-22 Raptors streaked across the sky over Boston Harbor. The squadron dove in diamond formation towards the Atlantic Ocean's depths to plane up, over and above the *U. S. S. Constitution*, "Ol' Ironsides," sailing to its berth at nearby Charlestown. The 'first-look, first-shot, first-kill,' capability of the jet fighters assured America's status, as: "the Land of the Free and the Home of the Brave."

The United States of America's flag, – "Old Glory," – 'the red, white and blue' has always been waived to honor the red blood of military heroes who have died fighting for the purity manifested by the white stripes of liberty and equality, beneath the starry blue skies of fought for freedom. The black silhouettes of the Raptors in the glowing yellow sun now precisely philosophized that same message: *"E Pluribus Unum!"*

First Nations, however, still speak, and often in the English language, of another protector and defender, an earth mother and a much earlier Symbol for their *Countrie*.

CHAPTER I.

GIVE BLOOD – implored the Red Cross sign blazing from the Donor Center's window, located on the outskirts of Chinatown. Philip Parkerman, a recent graduate in Art History (*Summa Cum Laude*) from nearby Harvard University, read the words as he did every morning on the way to his temporary job. Against the blithe September sky a few yellow leaves clung to the branches of a nearby Elm tree outside Boston's Beagle Bookshop. A cloth Beagle wearing big black-framed glasses appeared to browse amongst the books in the picture window of the red-brick building. The toy dog affectionately reminded him of many an Ivy League girl.

Chalked letters on a slate said: OPEN! With a glance at traffic he put his best foot forward and briskly strolled across the street. Brass chimes musically tinkled when he opened the shop door. Van Cliburn playing Brahms sounded from the speakers: *Waltz in A-Flat*. Philip noticed that there were already several customers perusing books. Mrs. Cohen, (Sadie) the owner's wife stood behind the cash register. Her maiden name Sarah Israel [after her mother of Bergen Belsen] had been a common name assigned to European Jewish orphans. A good-looking brunette, she too wore big, black-framed glasses, except hers held tiny diamonds in the corners. – "Good morning," chortled Philip, "*Shalom Aleichem!*"

Before she could reply, her daughter Rakel Cohen popped up and answered between gleaming, silver teeth-braces:

"We watched you as you procrastinated across the street, and we thought you were going to ditch work today."

"Rakel!" her mother said, barely repressing an outward expression of warmth for her precocious teenage daughter. "Nice girls don't say things like that." Turning to the young man, she said: "*Aleichem Shalom, Philip.*"

Philip loved Rakel. He had worked at the shop for almost two weeks and during that time he had fallen in love with the beautiful young girl. Her peers called her a J.A.P. (Jewish American Princess); and the golden Star of David on the platinum chain that she wore around her neck acknowledged her status like a badge of office. Now speechless, Philip wondered how could she suggest that he'd skip work? Why does she speak such cruel thoughts?

Interrupting his philosophical self-questioning, Sadie emphasized the words 'old' and 'new' while stating: "Mr. Cohen wants you to clear some space upstairs in the attic for a 'new' shipment of 'old' books. Rakel will go up later to help you."

"I'll supervise," said Rakel, as she put the attic key on the countertop. Pleased, she smiled, like Leonardo's Louvre masterpiece, *Mona Lisa,* the world's most popular portrait painting.

Philip gave a nod of affirmation, picked up the key and headed for the stairs. Along the wall hung prints of historic events in New England: an anonymous *Mayflower Pilgrims Landing,* a *Salem Witch Trial,* Paul Revere's engraving of the *Boston Massacre* and at the top of the stairs, Grandma Moses: *Bringing In The Maple Sugar.*

Dusky, the Beagle's attic, though a Bull's Eye window set in a far nook overlooking the street cast into the cobwebs and gloom a slanting shaft of sunlight, full of suspended dust particles. Many shelves and boxes of books later he had cleared a small spot near the rain-streak-stained windowpane. It had not been an easy job, and after only fifteen minutes the young man had worked up a sweat and his head ached. He coughed and sat down on a wooden box beneath the window. Pulling a white handkerchief from his pocket he wiped his brow. Suddenly his heart jumped. In the obscurity of the shadows on his left, he perceived the form of a figure like a missing link from the dim primordial past.

The mysterious creature stepped forth: – Rakel! She wore a surgeon's mask over her nose and mouth to protect her lungs from the dust; and a scarf covering her hair gave the impression of some Holy Madonna's veil, a harem girl, or a high priestess about to utter an esoteric prophecy concerning the future of humankind's spiritual evolution.

"Sitting down on the job, I see," she said. Philip laughed. This is a good time, he thought, to try the pet name he had heard her father use.

"Got to rest," he said. "It gets stuffy here, – Rocket."

"That's Rockette! Like the Rockefeller Center," she said wryly. "Oh, look! See how the sunshine streams forth like a Divine Light upon that chest over there!"

He looked to where she pointed. Sure enough. The sunlight shone onto an old battered footlocker-like trunk tucked away under a low shelf. Standing up he said impressively:

"Celestial radiance makes itself perspicacious, as though it should illumine a holy document, or something like that."

"Yeah," said Rakel, "What's in that box anyway?"

He dragged the dust caked container away from the

wall. "Hmm. Perhaps, we shouldn't disturb this? It looks old enough to be Pandora's," he said, making reference to Greek Mythology's first woman, who out of curiosity opened the box that released all human ills.

"I, I won't be upstaged, by her," Rakel said. "Open the box!"

Philip complied, saying:

"We won't surpass Napoleon's discovery of the *Rosetta Stone* in the Nile delta of Lower Egypt; and today in the British Museum, that *Stone* translated ancient Egyptian Hieroglyphics."

The young couple peered into the container. And behold! – a packet of paper tied together with a blue-ribbon faded to yellowish green, which also fastened a string of four glass beads and a little bird's feather. The bundle itself, several inches thick, rested atop a group of loose papers over a foot deep. Philip picked up the aged pack of bound, pale-brown pages and held them out to Rakel.

These are much older than the box," he said. "Probably over a hundred years old."

As she undid the threadbare ribbon, Philip noticed Rakel wore *blanc de Chine* fingernail polish, and he breathed her scent of *Chanel 'Mademoiselle'* perfume. The draft yielded inky scrawlings.

"What does it say?" she asked, her voice a whisper.

Philip replied, slowly reading: *The Legend of Karen Bluejeans!"*

"It's a manuscript?" Rakel asked.

"Let's see," he said, and he turned over the brittle, blotched brown title page and read. "Yes, it seems to be a Native American legend about a Mic-Mak Indian girl called Karen Bluejeans, during the French and Indian War, something like

James Fenimore Cooper's *Leather-Stocking Tales*, his novel – *The Last of the Mohicans*, 1826."

"Are these her legend too?" she asked, tapping the tip of her index finger upon the stack of loose papers.

After a few moments of looking through the box, he said: "Yes, I think those are different roots of the manuscript. After all it's a legend, and legends are added to or subtracted from depending on whose acquainting it, – how it gets put together, *etcetera*."

Thumbing through the papers, he said: This legend of Karen Bluejeans most likely began as oral tradition, and then it was written into the margin of another work, such as a family Bible. These papers could be copied from archives, both public and private, –or church parish records, minutes of rural town meetings, journals, diary entries, notes and a variety of other sources. Here's a page with French. And this has something in Latin."

He let the papers fall down into the box, and said: "Another probable consideration is that her legend was told originally with an Indian tongue, and then translated into English, then back to the Indian and so on. The story changed."

"You know Phil," Rakel said. "I think that this legend is going to be worth a lot of shekels."

She rubbed her fingers and thumb together, implying money. "Especially," she added, "if you're telling the story."

"Me?" he asked, holding his right hand over his heart like a sign of loyalty, as though pledging allegiance to the Stars and Stripes.

"Yeah, you!" said Rakel, untying her surgical mask and allowing it to fall down upon her breasts. She slipt off her scarf and pushed the back of her hair up onto her head. You've done all that research in Art History classes and everything. Tell us a bed-time story."

The scent of her expensive French perfume exquisitely overwhelmed his olfactory senses with pleasure. She let her hair fall down. And then she put her arms around his neck and kissed him on the mouth. For Rakel loved Philip.

The more they examined the papers the more Rakel realized that Karen Bluejeans had a story worth telling to the whole world, regardless of any future economic profit.

⁓

'Neath the Milky way, which they call, "the place where the stars river," – the Woodland Indians or Eastern Native Americans, Canada's Mi'kmaq or Mic-Mak (Children of the Dawn) have handed this tale down from generation unto generation. Around early autumnal campfires they remember the Indian girl called Karen Bluejeans. She has become an earth mother who yet gives birth to much of their concepts of freedom.

Blue smoke rises from orange and yellow campfire flames burning in the graying twilight air. Before *Boreas* (the North Wind) blows freezing snowflakes along the St. Lawrence River, the last soft warm breezes flow and confidentially murmur among reeds and willow-beds. An elderly shaman, the holy man, the magic maker shakes a gourd rattle filled with pebbles and chants. His female protégée toots a loon-bone whistle while dancing. Seeds make rhythm sounds within her turtle-shell ankle-bracelets. And for a moment the maple leaf flutters coyly like a lady's fan.

⁓

A small grayish-green Tree Frog only about two-inches large appeared on a flat rock at the water's edge, where freshwater from a little riverlet emptied into marshy weeds. The frog sang a slow musical call and then a faster higher-pitched trill like a flute's or the voice of a Red-bellied Woodpecker. It was rare for this frog to sing at river's edge except during mating season.

Through the freshwater side of the rock silently slithered a Northern Water Snake, thirty-inches long, and characterized with an adult's black neck spots, dorsal blotches and other markings. Poised, the snake reared its head and sprang forward to trap the frog in deadly jaws. On the flat rock gorged and satiated with his quick kill the pregnant snake exposed herself to unforgiving heavens.

Observing with bird's eye view, while with six-foot wing-span, soaring high overhead came the predator. From his perch on the azure rim of the world, the Bald-Headed Eagle fell, – like the javelin flung by the Mount Olympus King of the Gods: – like Zeus's thunderbolt! Sharp talons crushed the snake's head and the big bird flew away with his prey, the captured reptile's reflex reactions writhing. The eagle landed and perched on the branch of a gnarled tree growing out of a rocky cliff-side. One claw clutched to the tree limb while the other grasped the snake's head and fed the bird's biting beak. The serpent's body dangled down like a jungle vine. From their kayak, the Woodcutter with his six-months old, Timber-wolf sled-dog, *Wolf* had watched the snake-bearing eagle disappear over the horizon in New France's *Canada* (a name derived from the Iroquoian Huron word for "settlement" – *Kanata*).

"It's an omen," Josef said, to *Wolf.* Aloud he prayed: "St. Christopher, Patron Saint of Travelers carry us to safety just as you carried the Christ Child Jesus over the flooding river!"

A while ago Josef had visited the far North Country lands around *Baffin Bay* and he had gone *Eskimo* (or *Esquimaux*). That explained the kayak instead of a birch bark canoe, and his sailing sign painted at the prow: an arctic whale with a long, spirally-twisted ivory tusk – *The Narwhale*! He had chosen this creature to identify his kayak because the narwhale's tusk often resembled the cutting saw of a lumberjack or wood-cutter. The arctic association went well with Josef's new commercial image, the ever-resourceful *Inui*t or *Eskimo*. Back home in Quebec City his wife *Marie* like many of his friends already patronized him with his new nickname: "Eskimo."

Eskimo had been cruising this little estuary of the St. Lawrence quite a lengthy period; and he was beginning to worry that his vessel might get waterlogged, particularly if caught in another rainy down-pour. He spoke to *Wolf* whose head snuggle between Joseph's knees under the kayak's deck of sealskins. "We better put in at that little island and wait out this storm," he said, explaining, "the waterways will freeze soon, but there's no danger of that happening just yet." The sky was as dark and as gray as a Canada Goose. Towards a small wooded island, with his maple paddle, he steered their craft.

The gulf waters were full of life, all kinds of mammals and fishes, including seals, sharks and even whales. But now caution was required only for the potential dangers from tempest winds and waves, and the driving, freezing rains. Near the rocky evergreen-forest shoreline *Wolf* growled. Beached in the bulrushes, tangles of purple grapes and brambles of wild, climbing red roses: a doll-size dugout of Elmwood!

"What's this?" asked Josef, seizing his firearm. The rugged beauty of the scene hinted of *Satan's* sorcery. *Wolf* wiggled out from the kayak and jumped into the shallows. The long-legged creature leapt and barked at the tiny boat while the Woodcutter secured their own vessel at the water's edge.

"Archangel Michael, the Good Angels, Saints and Martyrs protect us!" Josef muttered, moving towards the cradle-like ark. He peered into the elfin ship. A papoose swathed upon a cherry cradle-board gurgled at him. The sun was carved above the infant's head, and beneath his feet in profile a beaver atop a turtle. A masterpiece of embroidered beadwork, the swaddling cloth displayed singing Robin Redbreasts, barking Foxes, and yellow, green and purple floral elements. Perfect bilateral symmetry indicated Mic-Mak origin.

Quickly Josef glanced around, fearing Indians to screech from the underbrush, tomahawk and scalping-knife thirsty for blood. Again Josef looked at the baby. He and *Marie* were unable to have their own children.

This is the son of a great Indian chief," he informed *Wolf.* Massaging the dog's ears, he said: "We cannot abandon the infant. Aside from savages and starvation, there are many perils such as wild beasts, predatory birds, bad weather, insects and other evils. Worst of all is *the Devil* and his *Demons.*"

He looked over his shoulder and said: "No. No, no. It's not sage for us to stay here. And the brave Indian Prince will surely expire if we don't take him with us."

Wolf grinned in agreement. Josef ordered his animal companion below deck, and then he grabbed the cradle-boarded baby and stuffed it too under the deck. *Wolf's* nose nudged the papoose. The dog would act as both big brother and baby sitter, – homeward bound. Removing a rosary from his pocket Josef went back to the dugout. For a trade offering and a blessing he hung the cross and wooden-beads on a twig over the baby's boat and quickly made the sign of the cross. Still afraid of a surprise Indian attack, he shoved off into the expansive, choppy water under the ominous, darkening clouds. *The Narwhale* sped off, as slick as an otter.

"Sweet Virgin *Marie,*" prayed Josef, paddling fiercely, "Mother of God, help us get back to Quebec City, and I will

carve a statue in devotion to your loving mercifulness." Such
an art work, known as a *De Voto*, was popular in New France.

Far below the trembling sky the sealskins-barque appeared
invisible. Thunder! Eskimo recalled hearing that for Mic-Mak
tribal tradition a clap of thunder was the release of the Great
Spirit's Bow. Suddenly a steak of lightning cracked the firmament, and heaven was illuminated! Heavy rainfall followed
the awful flash. Down the sea-lane's white-capped waves black
with seals, ploughed paddled *Narwhale*. Overhanging crests of
foam-heaps crashed, toppling and tumbling under the rain-
drenched sheets of wind that slapped the squall's salty spray.
Rowing voyaged the water-rider.

Quebec City existed as a castle in the sky, a magnificent fairytale metropolis in the early morning mists, or when
within his ken, so the City seemed to Josef wearily under way
to port. Down his cheek slid a teardrop of joy.

Founded in 1609 by *Samuel de Champlain*, atop the
steep 300-feet-high cliffs of *Cap Diamond* overlooking the
St. Lawrence River and called *Stadacone* or *Kebec* ('where the
waters narrowed') by Indian Chief *Donnacona*, the place had
grown into a Cathedral city, the fabled City of God on a Hill.
Palace, University, schools, hospitals and dwellings arose along
the skyline. Towers pinnacled with colorful pennants streaming, and steeples up-holding the Cross of Christ silhouetted
this summit of the New World's Jerusalem!

Now, in 1745, Quebec City reigned as the capital of New
France.

The French royal flag, the white and gold *Fleur-De-Lys*
waived from the City's parapets over most of North America:
from Canada's Hudson Bay in the far North and the Gulf of
the St. Lawrence, all the way to the Great Lakes and backwoods
and rivers, across the Great Plains to the rocky Mountains in the

West, and down the Mississippi River south through Louisiana to New Orleans on the Gulf of Mexico. Quebec City was the most precious jewel in the crown of France's *King Louis XV*. Ever since *Jacques Cartier*, the *St. Malo* navigator from *Brittany*, while seeking a Northwest Passage to the riches of the Far East, had named Canada (from the Indian word, *Kanata*, – "village, community"), *the City* had become a focal point of civilization.

Ding! Dang! Dong! The seminary's bells rang the morning-tide *Angelus*: Ding! Dang! Dong! After a night of un-relenting rain, drizzling day had broken. Josef climbed steps to *the City's* Upper Town (carved cradleboard and sleeping baby in his arms), like a Jew parading a Torah Scroll in a Synagogue on the Sabbath..

Bang! Bang! His fist pounded upon the wooden door.

"We've arrived!" announced Josef when *Marie* loomed in the doorway of their home, *White Owl's Nest*. Names instead of numbers identified locations in *the City*.

Marie's ancestors had built this townhouse long ago. The family saga boasted of Viking warrior descent, which accounted for her ice-blond hair, Scandinavian-blue eyes and *Thor*-like temper. She once told Josef that when she dies, *Odin* the Nordic creator and the *Valkyrie* his handmaidens will wel-come her in the heavenly hall of slain heroes – *Valhalla!*

Josef and *Marie* had lived in these few rooms since their wedding day twenty years ago. *Wolf* slept before the fireplace on a polar-bear rug that the Woodcutter had traded for at the same time that he had bartered to secure the pup. They met expenses and profited through Josef's contracts to provide fire-wood for the Governor's Palace and other important places..

"We'll put him here," said Josef, carrying the cradleboard baby to *Wolf's* space. "I'll build him a bunk. He was the son of a powerful chief."

"Josef!" said *Marie*, trying to get a kiss while seeing what it was that he carried. Both fists clenched, she demanded:

"What are you talking about?"

Josef cast one last carpenter's glance at the bunk space and replied: "We have been given a boy. The Blessed Mother has intervened for us. I've found a baby Prince in the reeds just like Moses in the Bible."

He turned the cradleboard towards *Marie*. The papoose peered out from behind the baby-blanket's folds. His face had been smeared with reddish-brown clay to protect him against bites from black flies and mosquitoes. Middle-aged and barren, *Marie* lacked only the love a child could bring. She uttered a cry.

"Oh, Josef! A son! How? Where are his parents?" Josef placed the cradleboard on the table and the new mother began to unfasten the infant's bedding. Exhausted from his journey, Josef poured water into a copper kettle hanging over the hearth fire that he could wash himself before sleeping.

"*Wolf* and I sought safety on an isle of pines, for the weather threatened our lives. We found the boy bravely guarding the place for us. I'll make him my partner. He will take care of you and me in our old age.

"*Wolf* is his friend already. They kept each other warm under *the Narwhal's* hides."

Suddenly *Marie* declared her own discovery.

"Look Josef. Look!" she cried: "It's a girl! We have a beautiful baby girl."

The foster father felt disappointed, but *Marie* emerged such as one so young and so lovely as she took care of the baby's needs that he laughed.

"I wonder what this means?" he said, "a furrow of white lilies a-bloom beneath a crescent moon," as deep as a nocturne, embroidered on the reverse of the baby's blue blanket. *Marie* held the sleeping baby and walked to the spread blanket to help analyze the images.

"These are symbols of purity," she said. "We'll call her Karen. Karen means purity."

I think we should include the blue background too," said Josef. "These blue cloths balance our present time with her older Mic-Mak origins. Let's call her Karen Blue-blankets."

"Oh, Eskimo," reasoned *Marie*, "these are more than mere blankets. This material is serge from southern France." She rubbed the material between her thumb and forefinger, and said: "Sailor's cloth!"

Marie's predecessor wasn't Leif Erikson, the noble son of Eric the Red who had reached Labrador and titled the "rocky land" – *Helluland*. Nor did her Norse ancestor discover Iceland, Greenland, Newfoundland, Vinland (Cape Cod) or Acadia. He may have been Norwegian or from Denmark, a seafarer Dane. Or he had been a Swedish seaman who had served in the French Merchant Marine and then settled in Normandy where *Marie's* maternal family came from. And since the days *Armand Jean du Plessis de Richelieu* received the red cap from Rome to become the influential *Cardinal Richelieu*, all persons in New France were required to be French and Catholic. Yet as the beautiful woman regarded the cloth she liked to pretend that it came from the booty of her real or imagined great-great-grandfather's Dragonship.

"Jeans is another name for serge," she said.

"Let's call her Karen Bluejeans."

"Karen Bluejeans," repeated Josef. "A very good name for a Mic-Mak girl adopted by French Canadians."

The baby having been washed and fed, slept on the bed. Softly *Marie* sang a soothing lullaby: "Rock a bye, baby, in the tree top . . . ." Eskimo embraced *Marie,* and in the light and the shadows of the fireplace's flickering flames they kissed each other again like young lovers.

Soon after, the baby was baptized by the same priest who had married them two decades earlier, a *Recollet* missionary, Father Greyrobe. He performed the Sacrament against the general wishes of Bishop *Francois Levele* and the rival Roman Catholic Order, the Society of Jesus or Jesuits, founded in Spain by *Saint Ignatius Loyola.* Through Vatican Jesuits instructed Christianity to China, Patagonia and other strange and distant lands, and they dominated the spiritual leadership of New France. Scorched with scalding water in mockery of baptism, and branded and burnt with heated red-hot axe heads, many Jesuit missionaries had met tortured martyrdom at the hand of the native. As a result they didn't approve of baptizing Indians until the last moment before death. The promise that Baptism gave eternal salvation in the happy hunting grounds of heaven helped enable the Jesuits to politically control the heathen savages.

Nevertheless, Father Greyrobe baptized the baby, "Karen Bluejeans," beneath, *God the Benevolent Creator,* Josef's woodcarving that hung suspended by chains above the altar in the Lower Town's *petite 'Holy Child Chapel'.* Carved in oak of dark, German Chocolate hue, this masterpiece was the flower of Josef's youth. Featured with long hair, a flowing beard, hands raised in blessing and a prayer shawl that blended into parting clouds, God smiled down upon all of His creation. The work was an art treasure of Quebec City. Father Greyrobe had encouraged the altarpiece and believed himself partially responsible for it, as part of his mission in New France, – "For the greater glory of God!"

Joan, a waitress friend of *Marie,* served as Godmother and

held the baby. *Jacques-Louis*, her husband worked in winter for Josef as a lumberjack, but now he was out in the wilds collecting beaver skins (as *coureur-de-bois,* or runner of the woods). His ideal trader was Dutchman *Peer Minuit* who had traded twenty-four dollars worth of glass beads for New York's island of Manhattan (twenty-two thousand acres) in 1626. In the absence of *Jacques-Louis*, Josef's boyhood friend and caretaker of the Ursuline Convent School, *Bonhomme Simon* stood in as proxy Godfather. During the ritual's ceremony he held the silver basin under the baby girl.

The priest poured the holy water and prayed: "I baptize thee Karen Bluejeans in the Name of the Father, His Son Christ Jesus and the Holy Paraclete." She was Christian now and not a pagan or some wild animal of the wilderness like the vixen, the she-bear or the doe.

Scented beeswax candles burned and the stained-glass rose-window reflected light bejeweling the blessed scene. Joan, who had always secretly coveted *Marie's* possessions, made sure that her two-years old son *Jacques-Pierre* acquired a reserve status as future husband to the Christian Mic-Mak girl. His baptismal gift, a Holy Card painted by Father Claude a century earlier, showed the saintly Indian Maiden: *Kateri Tekakwitha,* – "The Lily of the Mohawks."

◈

Outside the castle walls of Quebec City the world waged war. Canadian Cod fishing and commerce with France was jeopardized, and New France's fur trade was losing to developing, agricultural industriousness of Britain's North American colonies. Pirate Sir Francis Drake's friend, Sir Walter Raleigh had founded Virginia for the Virgin Queen, Elizabeth I, and several other colonies grew along the coast between the Atlantic Ocean and the Appalachian Mountains, as thorns in the side of France's Empire. When Massachusetts Governor Shirley and his militia of farmers, fishermen and mechanics took measures to defend the Commonwealth, Plymouth's pulpit preached that New England's Protestants had triumphed over the Pope's idol-worshipping Catholics.

On the continent, Charlemagne and the Holy Roman Empire's imperial vestige, Emperor Charles died without a son, but he left a legal document, the *Pragmatic Sanction* that guaranteed the Austrian succession to his eldest daughter, who became *the Empress Maria Theresa* of Austria's Hapsburg dynasty. When her state of Silesia was seized by King Frederick of Prussia, she threw all of her property into its defense, Hungary, Bohemia, Transylvania and more. And she rallied her sworn allies: Spain, Russia, Sweden and other European states. Prussia's Sword was mightier than the Book, Robe or Pen; Frederick maneuvered tens-of-thousands of soldiers and fiercely fired artillery (grape, shot and canister), as never seen before in warfare. Later Britain joined Prussia against France and Austria.

In Scotland, the Stuart Heir, Jacobite – "*Bonnie Prince Charlie*," (the Young Pretender) bid to take the British throne from the lawful King of England, German House of Hanover's George II. Suffering defeat, a sorry Charlie, disguised as a woman escaped back to France. His highlanders were slaughtered on the killing fields of Culloden Moor by the King's son, William Augustus, the Duke of Cumberland – 'the Butcher,' who crushed the rebellion with the order: "No quarter given!" Lieutenant Jack Wales of the Royal Marines served with the Navy's transporting of troops and supplies by sea to battle sites. His friend, Major James Wolfe, a staff officer demanded fresh meat for the troops. Both officers had served with the Duke in

Germany. Though Wolfe stayed in Scotland for pacification duties, peace-keeping police work and construction of roads, he had confided to Jack:

"I'd rather return to Germany and enter the cavalry." Seventeen years old, a year younger than Wolfe, Jack replied:

"I'm going on loan with the East India Company. I'll sail the route of the Portuguese *Vasco Da Gam*a and *Prince Henry the Navigator via* Africa's *Cape of Good Hope.* Journey to the subcontinent begins tomorrow."

Yet, tomorrow is a long time. From Hampton Roads in southeast Virginia, *Jove* a big heavyweight black slave left with his master's son for Boston . And on the south side of the St. Lawrence, in the backwoods frontier of New England tomorrow would never come for settler Stephen Cronath. French-Canadian Indians had crept out of the rainy dawn and devastated his farm. Painted and be-feathered, waving torches, shooting guns, burning and yelping like fiends from the Jaws of Hell, the Red Devils hit homestead hard. Then stealing whatever they wanted that proved easy to handle, the savages nonchalantly drifted into the forest.

Fortunately, the settler's wife and daughters had gone over the hills and far away in answer to their kin's invitation 'come over and help us' prepare for Thanksgiving Day. They would have been held as captives for ransom, the Red Man's white slaves! Mark, the settler's son had driven the wagon of womenfolk just before the storm. On his way back home he saw a column of black smoke rising in the sky. His heart offered an upright, 'appeal to heaven', like the summit of a tall pine tree, or like one of the many white church steeples in the New England countryside directing prayer heavenward. On-and-off fighting along the frontier for over a hundred years had fed fuel for the fires of terror at Indian attack.

Armed with his blunderbuss (a Puritan relic from his grand-father's era) loaded to fire, his momentary hope sunk like an anchor, as he approached the farm just before twilight on the day of the raid. Curled up in front of the charred ruins of the family's cabin his father's body had shrunk from loss of blood and body fluids. Dark stains covered the man's chest where a bullet had entered his rib cage near his heart. A second bullet had been fired at close range into his father's head above the temple of the right eye. Coagulated black blood resembling clumps of poisonous berries called attention to a killer's cold-blooded act of homicide. Mutilation had followed. The settler had been scalped and left to rot for the dogs, wild animals and birds of prey. The boy felt weak, like the wind had been knocked out of him. From the wagon he staggered back carrying an old elk hide with which he covered his father. Burial later. First he had to look around. *Molly*, the brown milk-cow's throat was slit from ear to ear. Hunks of her body had been hacked out for meat. A bad job too. She had suffered greatly to die. Flies were feasting on the exposed parts of her carcass. The savages had probably killed her for the missing metal cowbells she had worn. He fought down a tearful choke in his throat as he remembered how his young sisters affectionately hung the rustic musical instruments around the bovine's neck that she shouldn't get lost in the woods.

Prudence, the pregnant, sandy-colored sow was dead too. Mice and ants ate from her purple-mottled, pinkish underbelly ripped open, apparently while she was still alive. Succulent foetal piglets had been torn from her. The runt with a piece of swine intestine poked into its mouth had been kept inside the mother hog, Indian witchcraft to make sure that future pigs should grow fat for good hunting!

Injuns are cruel, he thought. Everything was gone. None

of the chickens or anything remained. The cornfields and wheat stacks were only damaged because the rain had spared them from total destruction by fire. The Indians had been too indolent to gather up the crops.

"Injuns are lazier than niggers," he said aloud.. The boy knelt down next to his father and wept. And then rising to his feet, Mark Cronath sobbed his new creed, a personal code to live by:

"I'll kill every Indian alive," he swore upon the dead body of his father. "The only good Indian is a dead Indian!"

Night fell hard and fast like a sharp axe splittin' wood.

CHAPTER II.

"God gave Canada to France!" Bishop *Levele* spoke emphatically to the girl students of the Ursuline Nuns Convent School. This exclusive educational institution was founded in Quebec City's Upper Town by *Madame de la Peltrie* over one-hundred seventeen years ago, in 1636. Two years later, *Marie Guyard* (who by mystical visions had received Divine Revelation) became the school's first superior – Mother *Marie de l' Incarnation*.

Through the courtyard gate just off *Parloir* street passed the privileged daughters of *habitants* (citizens, like Josef, born in Canada), as well as the daughters of new colonists from France, and Canadian Indian girls. Nuns taught the children to become good wives and mothers through Religion, French, Art, Parisian Manners, bathing, dressing, and practical homemaking skills, such as cooking, sewing, knitting and embroidery. Bernadette, the eldest student might hear the calling, "to take the Veil," and join the Order.

This year 1754, there were fourteen white girls ranging from age nineteen down to one pretty, blonde-haired child of three years, and ten little Indians. To discourage snobbery brought about by expensive and fashionable clothes the girls all wore the same kind of uniform, brown jumper with a white blouse, black apron and black knee-socks, and in cool weather a pale gray sweater. Brown shoes that laced up six-inches above the ankle were worn, and older girls were allowed high heels of an extra two-inches. Three white girls boarded at the school since their families lived too far away for daily commute.

Other day students lived in Quebec City or nearby, and most walked to school. Patricia traveled daily to and fro in a carriage drawn by four dappled mares. All of the Indians boarded except nine-years old Karen Bluejeans who lived at *White Owl's Nest*, almost around the corner from the Convent. *Red Feather*, only six years old sat behind her on the Virgin Mother's side of the Cathedral *Notre Dame des Victoires*, while the Bishop taught them. Beside him resting upon an easel, a large oil painting illustrated the theme of his talk.

"We begin at the top of the picture, just as a painter paints a wall so that any unintentional paint-drops drip down onto untouched surface. At the uppermost part of the painting God and Virgin Mother *Marie* sit upon celestial thrones hovered over by clouds of Good Angels. All is radiant glory and rainbow brilliance. Beneath them in rows arranged like seats at the Paris Opera sit the Apostles, Saints, Old Testament Prophets and Canadian Martyrs." The Bishop gazed at the painting silently for a few seconds then raised his hands in surprise.

"Oh, look! Who is this teenage girl? *Marie Magdelaine de Vercheres!* – Canada's own blond heroine." The instructor held his hands clenched in fists at his throat, and loudly enunciated:

"Liberty? Nay. Life! Life itself was at stake. She rallied the defense of her village, *Castle Dangerous*. Against attacking British Iroquois she fought until her father arrived with French soldiers to save the day. She too appears here in the honor gallery of the righteous." He lifted his hand again, as though presenting the painting anew. "*Marie de Verchere's* cameo appearance portraits an example of what you can expect from Paradise. A reward for Christian self-sacrifice in the service of King and Country: a place in Heaven." The Bishop stopped talking and regarded the painting and acquiesced his approval to the girls. The lecture continued.

"Halfway down the canvas, robed in dark blue velvet hemmed with ermine and decorated with silver-white, *Fleur-De-Lys*, stands the crowned figure of *King Louis XIV*, the embodiment of France. Uplifted, his right hand's forefinger points to the sky and Heaven's Court; his left hand rests upon the head of a kneeling native Indian, at the bottom of the painting."

Levele assumed the position of the painting's French King, with uplifted finger.

"At the King's feet kneels an Indian Chief. This noble savage personifies Canada. France has bestowed French-Catholic Civilization upon Canada. Behind our Sovereign, to his right a Royal Galleon floats upon the St. Lawrence River, France – as the Ship of State presiding over earthly affairs upon 'the river of life'. On the left of the Monarch, towering cliffs rear upward in domination at the top of the world – Quebec City! And let us not neglect to notice that at the foot of these cliffs in the background a Jesuit priest blesses the scene: "God gave Canada to France!"

The lecturer momentarily posed like the priest in the picture.

The art work had vividly displayed the essence of the Bishop's message. No cause to confuse the viewer existed. He paced back and forth in front of the three pews of girls. Suddenly he halted, raised his eyes upward and then looked at the students.

With out-held hands he implored their absolute attention.

"God Almighty gave Canada to France. Canada's mountains and forests, rivers and lakes, birds and fishes, the beaver and other fur-bearing animals, even the rocks and minerals and Indian peoples. All of Canada's wealth and beauty unto France, Our Lord God has given."

The Bishop looked down at the floor in deep concentration. He stared hard at the girls.

Each one wore a black skull-cap as a sign of piety, except Bernadette who wore a short, black veil. How could he make them understand? Dressed in purple and scarlet, he stood lean and tall. His thin lips and the corners of his mouth exhibited a dryness as though he had never laughed; nor ever had wine enjoyed.

"My dear children in Christ, do you understand? God gave Canada to France, that France should rule the wilderness and teach the Red Heathen the words of Our Savior Jesus Christ."

Karen Bluejeans, the same as any of the other students listened to the Bishop's teachings.

"Does *the Devil* dwell on earth?" asked Canada's highest-ranking clergyman. Sitting in the second row, Gizelle, an attractive girl of sixteen years raised her hand to indicate that she knew the answer.

Bishop *Levele* ignored her and answered his question in a hushed manner.

"Yes, *the Devil* on hoof inhabits the earth. *The Devil* reveals himself as King of England!"

Gizelle pulled down her hand.

"Put simply – *The Devil* is the King of England," said the Bishop quickening his pace and increasing the volume of his voice. "He squats upon the British Throne in his own filth, fleas and vomit, threatening with his pitchfork. Gluttony,

greed, hatred, lust and envy consume him. Against the Ninth
Commandment, England's King covets Canada, – the country
that God gave to France!"

The Jesuit's sermon took on a confidential tone, but Karen
Bluejeans had lost her focus.

Instead she was thinking of her dog. She had started to
consider *Wolf* the moment she had heard the word 'fleas'
that allegedly hovered around England's King on the British
Throne. *Wolf* didn't like insects and she tried to keep them
off of him. That was part of her responsibility as a dog owner.

When she was a baby and a little girl, *Wolf* took care of her.
But now she was older. She was nine years old and her father
said that at most *Wolf* could only have the intelligence of a
seven-years-old boy. Now she had to take care of the big dog.

He was four feet tall like his mother, a timber wolf. But
Karen Bluejeans was taller by a foot and seven inches. Yet
Mother Superior refused to allow *Wolf* within the Ursuline
courtyard. There the girls gathered in pairs or groups to talk
or to play jump-rope and hopscotch, until Sister *Marie Anne*
rang the hand-bell, ring-a-ling-dinging time for commence-
ment of classes.

Last year he had walked Karen Bluejeans to school, but
that simply wasn't allowed anymore. So *Wolf* went to Beaver
Lodge, the work-yard where her father kept cords of wood and
tools and supplies. The site located near the place the apoth-
ecary Louis Herbert (the first French citizen of Canada) had
established his farm. There *Wolf* played with *Belle*, the Musk
Ox, who slept in the barn, with *Alex* and *Heloise*, the two
donkeys. *Belle* got rich with buttermilk. Inuit had traded both
Wolf and *Belle* at the same time in the North Country. Then
after *Quebecers* started to call Josef *l' Arbre*, the Woodcutter,
by his nickname, Eskimo [*L' Esquimau*].

Her father's head man, Larry Pena, 'the Golden Man' from 'Inca Land', supervised the animals and lumber work. He had journeyed from Peru, because Quebec City's river had his name, Lawrence. He felt that that should bring him good luck and fortune.

Don Juan 'Balboa' Ortiz worked the hay fields (alfalfa, barley, timothy) and vegetable gardens (carrots, peas, corn, beans, melon, pumpkins, squash, cabbages, rice), wheat, hemp, tobacco, flowers, apple orchard, grape vines, hedges of berry bushes and the lane of nut trees (walnut, hazel nut and chestnut). Rumor alleged Ortiz had fled Mexico after killing an *hombre* in a knife fight for love of *Maria Dolorosa*. Her lips tasted sweeter than *Cantina tequila*. Both Pena and Ortiz were Spanish speaking, illegal aliens; though not French, they were Catholic, and unlike French Protestant *Huguenots*, they were tolerated. Josef protected them from arrest.

Each year Beaver Lodge, near *Sainte Foy* Road, got bigger and better. Nonetheless, her mother insisted that the family must live in their townhouse *White Owl's Nest* in Quebec City's Upper Town, and not at *Chanticleer*, Beaver Lodge's stone farmhouse with the gold *Coq* weathervane atop the steep roof designed to slide off snow.

So sometimes *Wolf* stayed home with her mom, who babied him and always fed him treats. And that was precisely why he was getting fat. Karen Bluejeans told herself that today after school she would take her dog for a run along the cliffs overlooking the river, on Abe Martin's fields, the Plain of Abraham. *Wolf* really liked to run there. Of course that was asking for ticks and bug-bites. We'll play ball. He enjoyed playing fetch the ball. He had a new leather ball about as big as an apple; *Marie* had thrown away his old one because it was too mangled and overly-slobbered upon.

She looked up to the Bishop and realized a silence. Had he asked her a question? Was everybody waiting for her answer? A few of the nuns had philosophically put her with the white girls, as the adopted daughter of white people. She didn't board at school like the other Indian girls. Now they would call her stupid and ignorant. Those bad words most of the white girls had called the Indians whenever mistakes were made. Karen Bluejeans wanted to be a nice girl like the Virgin Mother that all the girls should be her friends. She burned with shame. But wait! The Bishop was pacing. Again he began to his talk.

"The Jews are guilty! *Jews* and *Demons* in British Parliament vote against us. All of the Maleficent Spirits plot there: *Satan, Diablo, Lucifer, Belial, Beelzebub, Azazel, Mephistopheles, the Old Serpent, Old Scratch, Old Poker, Puck*, and all other scamps, rogues, buggers and Hell's imps." Bishop *Levele* put his open hands near his mouth as though he were shouting:

"They conspire to crucify the King of France, as they've killed the Lord Jesus. The British Government will not permit peace in New France until the King of England with his spikey horns and pointy red tail can count Canada as his own." He glared at the girls.

"A nation is only as strong as its women!" He hesitated for a moment that the students should think about what he had just said. And then he proceeded: "To you young women of the Ursuline Nuns goes the duty of guarding our land and our own *King Louis XV*. God has given you this task just as God has given Canada to France. Pray for strength to serve as our strong, strong back-bone. Fight like *Marie Magdelaine de Vercheres*, and win your place in Heaven."

The girls knelt and in Latin he blessed them, concluding: "Go forth in the Grace of God." The Bishop retired through a door in the sanctuary. Sister *Marie Claire* came forward and stood before the students, her hands folded, and said:

"Alright girls, we'll leave the Cathedral and return back to school in single file as a group of young ladies and not like a gaggle of geese. Remember you're wearing your uniform and you represent the Ursuline Convent School; therefore let's not have any silly dawdling. You've just received our Bishop's blessing, so act accordingly." She stood at the end of the side aisle and said, "Bernadette will lead us."

Bernadette genuflected (crossing herself, since the Blessed Sacrament was in the Tabernacle) and departed through a side door. The next girl followed suite and all of the others thereafter. Karen Bluejeans was last in line for she had let young *Red Feather* cut in front of her. Each girl moved with awareness of her own carriage, shoulders back and head held high, eyes lowered and attention given to watch one's step. Inside the courtyard the young Nun announced a surprise:

"Mother Superior asked me to inform you that afternoon classes are cancelled. The rest of the day is a holiday!" She clapped her hands and made shooing noises as though the girls really were geese. Laughing cheerfully they shuffled off singly or in small groups. Sister waved them away like a chamber orchestra conductor waving a baton. Karen Bluejeans stayed a second longer than the others to say good-bye to *Red Feather*.

"I'll see you in the morning," she said. "I'm going to run *Wolf*, the fatty dog." Both girls giggled.

From a second-story window overlooking the courtyard, Mother Superior *Marie Etienne* observed the two Indian girls. To share the suffering of Jesus, beneath her habit she wore a hair shirt that scratched and irritated her skin. Sometimes using a knotted-rope she performed deep flagellation until she felt a frenzied sort of erotic pleasure.

That scarred and welt-bruised flesh on her back. Her diary revealed that her secret desire was to suck the penis of Jesus Christ during His Crucifixion to ease His pain. Nonetheless, she figured that Karen Bluejeans and *Red Feather* should be separated so that they both could better develop well-rounded personalities.

"Good-Bye," in Indian sign-language, said *Red Feather*. Karen Bluejeans replied in the sign-language that the younger girl had been teaching her. Both girls laughed. Then *Red Feather* joined the other boarders who had already roamed into the Dining Room for their lunch. Karen Bluejeans reminded herself not to run while wearing her uniform, or an unlady-like reputation might get cast upon the Convent School and the instruction of the Ursuline Nuns. Nevertheless, she did hurry home to *White Owl's Nest*.

"Don't slam the door!" her mother yelled, as the child rushed into the house. *Wolf* barked and she hugged him with love and affection.

"I'm here boy," she said. "We'll play together all day."

"First change your clothes," said *Marie*. "Put on your red shirt with the hood. That looks cute and neatly balanced when you're wearing your hair in braids like today. Then help me take these trays of meat pies down to your Godmother on Market Street. Many people are in *the City* today for summer is a-comin'."

The girl changed into red shirt, faded dungarees, and calf-high moccasins, and then ate lunch: French bread buttered with honey and goat's cheese, a bowl of strawberries in fresh cream and a handful of blueberries. Her mother sat at the kitchen table, but did not eat. *Marie's* face was flushed.

"Are you sick?" asked Karen Bluejeans. "What ails thee, my mother? Your face is wet."

"It's nothing," the mother replied, wiping her face with the shoulder of her blouse; drenched with perspiration, she continued: "I'm only hot from baking those meat-pies all morning."

About once a month whenever her mother got snared birds, trapped mice, stoats, rats, squirrels or any other rodent or small, meat creatures she made meat-pies that sold for a worth-while commission at lunchtime in the booth outside the restaurant, *La Roc*.

"They're only a few mouthfuls," Godmother Joan had said, holding up her thumb, "but they sell like hot cakes."

When *Marie* and Josef first married, the meat-pies money helped the household budget, but now Eskimo didn't want her to bake them. He knew that he earned more than enough money for their family. Yet she continued to prepare the tasty morsels. Her profit-making baking was an act of women's independence.

Francois Bigot, the *Intendant* (New France's Manager and Quebec City's Chief of Police) was second in authority only to the *Governor Pierre Francois Rigaud, Marquis de Vaudreuil*, and sometimes subordinate to Bishop Levele. *Bigot* did not allow much buying and selling without his approval. He cheated government and the people for his own pocket. Josef and Beaver Lodge were tolerated only because they assured firewood for the office of the *Intendant*.

"This morning's meals were extra," *Marie* said. "A boy from the docks brought me two brown creatures like big muskrats, trapped onboard one of the ships at sunrise. She raised an eyebrow and nodded affirmatively. "I cut them up into bacon bits, threw in some onions and salt, and baked them.

"Mmm! Sounds like I should sample one," said Karen Bluejeans.

"No!" said her mother loudly. "A girl sells her goods when

she's got them. You can't profit if you spoil your opportunities by compromising your wares."

"Oh, yes, mother," replied the dutiful daughter. "Please, lie down and cool off."

"Put a towel in between the trays, and one on top, too," said, *Marie*.

Karen Bluejeans did as told and set forth towards the Lower Town. Grinning like a Husky sled-dog, *Wolf* walked beside her.

Across the street some soldiers were escorting an American hostage, Scotchman Major Robert Stobo, who had been sent to ensure release of French prisoners. The Virginian, militia leader Major George Washington witnessed *Half-Chief*, a *Mingo* Indian ally, smash open the skull, wash his hands in blood and eat the brains of the French commander *Sieur de Julmonville*. The French & Indian War had unofficially begun! After one third of his forces had died of injuries, disease, rain, and lack of food and ammunition, Washington surrendered his make-shift Fort Necessity in a clearing called Great Meadows down by the confluence of the *Ohio, Allegheny* and *Monongahela* Rivers. Regarded as a murderer by many of the enemy, he was afforded full military honors as he led the armed Americans away back towards Williamsburg to the music of drums and fifes, – Colours Flying.

Karen Bluejeans regarded Stobo, the gentleman prisoner with curiosity more than fear or suspicion. While in Boston, Massachusetts, Pastor Reverend Woolen Mathers purchased the Virginia Negro named *Jove* and emancipated him – Abel Freeman. The son of *Jove's* master sold the black man rather than take him to Europe, where the boy was running away.

Along the steps of Mountain Hill Street crowds of people jostled and shoved. In the market place the girl almost dropped the trays of meat pies when a small green monkey leapt from one booth railing to another in front of her. He had swung with his arms. She had never even heard of a monkey before this and suddenly she was seeing one swinging. She was fascinated.

Wolf charged barking and snarling as he perceived the strange little beast; but the monkey spun around and around loop-dee-loop from the booth's highest railing. *Wolf* barked again. He could have jumped up and probably knocked down the entire booth, but he only barked.

"Quiet! Mongrel," cried an old, hunchbacked crone wearing round, silver ear-rings. "Shut your mouth or I'll slit open your throat." A stranger, she gave *the Evil Eye*.

"Hey, leave my dog alone!" Karen Bluejeans said boldly. "Can't you see he's barking at that – the green thing?" Her hands full with the trays she pointed at the tiny monkey with her chin. Close at her side *Wolf* gave a low growl from deep within this throat.

A tall, handsome man of dark skin came between the two females. He wore a ruffley, white shirt opened to mid-chest, and blue pantaloons with a faded, red satin sash wrapped around his waist. Black knee-high boots and a loop ear-ring of gold completed his costume.

"May I help?" he inquired, with the same foreign accent as the woman's, partially French and partially Spanish, and something else too. He had a thin, mustache with greasy, pointed ends.

"We are Gypsies from the South of France," he said. They were gypsies from *the Basque Country*, a dark region in the Pyrenees Mountains between the border of France and Spain. The Gypsy originated from somewhere deep in India. Then either by way of the area around the Black Sea to Romania and its vampire heartland, or across North Africa to *Catalonia* on the Iberian Peninsula, they migrated into Europe. Honest people distrusted gypsies as knife-throwing thieves, kidnapers, murderers and fortune-telling dealers of black magic. The green monkey climbed down onto the Gypsy's hand and shoulder.

"What is that?" asked, Karen Bluejeans, "some kind of squirrel?"

"I call it a monkey," said the man. "Kung! He comes from Brazil in South America. We, we obtained him at a stop in Panama; our ship arrived here this morning from Havana, Cuba. We don't stay long. Perhaps, you offer us food?"

Suddenly the trays of meat-pies seemed heavy. The Gypsy took a pie and gave it to the old woman. She sought another and then another. He took two for himself and one for Kung. Two more disappeared. Eating the pie like a sandwich, he said, "Delicious." Karen Bluejeans heard another low guttural growl from within *Wolf's* throat. She was pretty sure that earlier the big canine could have knocked over the booth supporting the monkey, but the dog was well-behaved when with her. She felt that she might trade the already eaten pies for King, or Kung or whatever it's called.

"How much do you want for the monkey?" she asked.

"How much money you got?" replied the Gypsy.

Well, I don't have any money," said Karen Bluejeans, "I have only these pies that my mother baked and that I'm taking to market."

"We'll taste a few more," he said and helped himself to three, – four pies. The whole top tray was empty, now. He handed the pies to the old woman.

"Monkey is not for sale," he said smiling. "What else you got to offer?" The monkey quit chattering and jumped up onto the booth railing again and spun another loop-dee-loop, like a kind of circus trapeze-artist.

"How does he do that," asked the girl fascinated, her eyes wide open with wonder. "How can he jump like that?"

"I train him to jump," answered the man. The aged woman dressed in black except for a red bandana tied around her head said something in a strange and not unmusical language. The man reached to remove the top tray, but Karen Bluejeans sidestepped behind *Wolf.* The sled-dog-like beast held his ground and snarled, showing sharp, white fangs. The Gypsy backed down. The Gypsy woman took one step forward. She put her foot down. She pointed a crooked finger at the young girl while the big dog barked.

"I curse thee! Death befall your mother!" croaked the sinister figure. "Maybe now you will not hesitate to share your dumplings?" She cackled.

Karen Bluejeans hurried away to *Le Roc* restaurant on the other side of Market Square. *Wolf* pressed against her leg. They left the pies with a waiter and headed back for the Upper Town.

The Gypsy woman regarded them until they had blended into the crowd going up the stairs of Mountain Hill Street. The Gypsy woman spat onto the ground where Karen-Bluejeans and *Wolf* had stood. For 'Bad Luck' to befall the girl, the Gypsy man spit over his left shoulder onto where the shadow of Karen Bluejeans had been laid out beneath the early afternoon sun. He leashed the monkey's neck. The hideous looking old hag sang some ancient, sing-song sound, as the Gypsies dilly-dallied back to the Saint Charles River docks.

Karen Bluejeans kept thinking about the monkey. She didn't know that it was a *Woolly Spider Monkey* from the tropical rainforests around *the Amazon River*. It would have been

larger and yellowish-gray instead of undersized, but its growth
was probably stunted from early confinement within a cage.
Chlorophyll from living fungus had caused the fur to appear
green. Specialized shoulder bones allowed arboreal locomo-
tion or swinging from one branch to another by its arms.
'Semibrachiation' is the term used to explain that this sort of
monkey often uses its tail too, as a kind of third arm when
running upon tree limbs or swinging. The little creature was
a primate like all humankind. When man came down from
the trees and began to walk erect with his hands free for tools
he evolved into a more complex-thinking organism.

At the *Saint Louis Gate*, she forgot about the monkey.
She produced *Wolf's* ball from her pouch and threw it as far
as she could. He ran down the leather orb and brought it
back to her. Over and over again they repeated this play. *Wolf*
streaked across the open fields and Karen Bluejeans pursued
him through the green sprouts of grass blades, the stubble of
weedy vegetation and the shrunken shrubs. Next he raced after
her. She couldn't dodge the timber-wolf. And that is what he
was, for when he ran his tail was straight, the trait of a wolf; a
dog's tail curdled upward. He caught her every time she tried
to get away. When it was her turn again to catch him, he let her
grab him. They wrestled together in the luxuriant, long grass.

The afternoon neared sunset when *Wolf* ran along the edge
of the cliffs above the river. He stopped, turned up his nose
and howled to the sky, challenging her to follow him. She did
and laughing threw her arms around him and hugged him
and petted him. The two of them sat down to rest. She sat
upon a small log with her arm around *Wolf.* The setting sun,
mellow-golden, passed behind clouds emitting rays of silver
radiance and intimating glory. A loud thunderclap warned
of rain.

'Great Thunderbird has flapped his wings', she said, thinking of the Mic-Mak myth, which featured an enormous bird, a common denominator among all Native Americans, especially the Southwestern Indians just above *the Rio Grande River*, as well as Great Raven's totem-pole tribes of the Pacific Northwest Coast. They headed home. Night came through gaps in the clouds, as constellations twinkled stars in the sky. Points of their reflection sparkled in the river. A black cat crossed her path. *Wolf* roared a warning but refused to reduce his dignity by giving chase to the jinx.

"I hope mother won't be angry about the pies," she said to herself, as she wearily returned to *White Owl's Nest*. *Jacques-Pierre*, sitting on the front steps, was playing a Jew's Harp. He walked up to her and they kissed each other's cheeks. He was two years older, but she was a few inches taller. A student at the seminary school, every evening he visited her. Saturday he labored at Josef's work-yard, and on Sunday he usually spent the afternoon with the boss's daughter and her pet *Wolf*, who tolerated the boyfriend. *Jacques-Pierre* held both of her hands together in front of her and looked into her dark-eyed beauty.

"Karen Bluejeans," he said solemnly, "You're mother is dead. Josef has taken her body to *Hotel-Dieu*, the General Hospital morgue. You're supposed to come back with me to my house."

Rain began to sprinkle. He put his arms around her, and whispered into her ear, "I'm sorry."

❧

CHAPTER III.

"All is illusion! Upon the 'Ocean Of Life' only *nothingness* is real," said Jack Wales, to his friend James Wolfe. "For true Buddhist Enlightenment you must overcome all human desires. Then through transcendental meditation you will experience the blissful peace of the farther shore, – *Nirvana*. It's synonymous with immortality." Jack's thick, black hair looked heroic.

"Immortality?" questioned Wolfe. They were having a drink and playing chess at an outdoor café in the *Latin Quarter* on the other side of the *Seine River*, across from France's *Notre Dame Cathedral of Paris*. "All I wish for myself is that I may at all times be ready and firm to meet that fate we cannot shun, and to die gracefully and properly when the hour comes," said James.

Wolfe had been presented at *Versailles* in an audience before France's *King Louis XV* and his politically-powerful mistress *Madame Pompadour, Jeanne-Antoinette Poisson,* the finishing touch to his sojourn abroad where he had cultivated his social grooming with Equestrianship, Fencing, French, Drawing and Dancing. He had served in the military since he was thirteen years old, and he should go back home soon as a Lieutenant Colonel. His father, a Marine General had purchased the promotion for the only living son; Edward the youngest boy had died fighting in combat alongside James in Germany years ago.

"*Dharma*, belief in Reincarnation! Transmigration of the soul. You're born again in another body, depending on your *Karma*, on how you lived your life," Jack continued. "Death is part of a cosmic cycle of regeneration and rebirth, – re-intergradation within the Great Mandala!"

Jack had just arrived from London where he had enjoyed a hero's welcome for displaying extreme valor. Clive of India defended *Arcot* against the French; *Mahomet Ali* was put on the throne restoring British power in the *Carnatic*. Jack had served Clive and Company as military advisor. Robert Clive, a Shropshire lad, went to India at age of eighteen, as a clerk for the East India Company. He took command of the company's military force and earned a reputation for courage. After driving off a final desperate assault by elephants wearing battle-armor, Clive won the name, *Sabut Jung* (the daring in war). Jack, a natural athlete, worked then after, wherever the Company sent him in the Far East.

Years later, the treasure ship *Golden Fawn* departed from the waters of South China's junk trade in opium. Sailing for home her officers and most of the crew had been struck dead by the Bubonic Plague. Devout *Hindus* had surmised that the disease's pox carried on the wind from *Sri Lanka* in exchange for human souls. Margaret, the King's niece had been aboard, as had large chests of gold bullion and several barrels of jewels, – emeralds, rubies, sapphires and Oriental pearl. The surviving crew entertained her with song, fiddles, pipes & tambourines, – dance music for Hornpipe, Jig & Reel, every evening that the weather permitted. The royal relative did not perish; nor were the Company's riches lost.

Jack had assumed command of the vessel and sailed it within sight of the White Cliffs of Dover. 'Twas a great accomplishment for any naval officer with knowledge of charts, sailing directions, log book, rose-card compass, sextant, the new chronometer and other eighteenth-century navigational devices; but it was a semi-miraculous trump for Jack, a Royal Marine and not an experienced sailor at all, except for a little sail-boating during his youth off the blithe and clouds studded, wave-crashed, slag-like rock-crags strewn along the coasts of Cornwall.

With the help of Billy 'Boy' Jones, a sailor lad from Bristol, he taught himself to sail the ship in the Indonesian Archipelago where they fortunately did not encounter pirates who preyed upon Spanish galleons and East India Company ships heavy with cargoes of peppers, cloves, ginger, cinnamon and other units of wealth. Neither mermaid nor giant, pea-green, dragon-like sea-serpent obstructed the ship's passage, though both characters had been outlined in Indigo ink and water-colored upon, 'the Master of Oceans' map. In the English Channel, a coast guard cutter took the ship to safety. The London Gazette coined the nickname: "*Union Jack*," Wales. Twenty-seven years old, he was promoted to the rank of major. King George II shook his hand in gratitude for rescuing his niece.

Jack placed his forefinger upon the Red Queen. He knew that Wolfe's parents had dis-couraged marriage to Miss Elizabeth Lawson, daughter of Sir Wilfred Lawson (Member of Parliament), and niece of General Mordaunt, an influential officer with the Horse Guards. She had been Maid of Honor to the Princess of Wales, also; but she had had not enough money to appease the expectations of Wolfe's mother.

"How are the Parisian women?" Jack asked, asked, moving the Queen upon the board.

Wolfe smiled and then laughed outright at Jack's blatant attempt at subtlety, the bringing up of the female element into the conversation just as he moved the Queen piece. Jack laughed, too.

"I find French women well bred, delicate and genteel, but they eat too much," Wolfe replied. "They've got indigestion too often." One coquettish mademoiselle had reported Wolfe as, 'bookish and responsible for her boring evenings'.

"How do you like the Rook?" Jack asked, changing the subject. They were playing with the chess set that Jack had brought back from India, as a gift for James: "Elephant-&-Castle!"

"Hannibal crossing the Alps," said Wolfe. "I've read that no great general played chess like a Grand Master. Chess and real world warfare don't mix well." Jack too would soon travel home. Horace Walpole, a London politician known for his use of words had summarized the political situation: "A volley fired from a young Virginian [George Washington] in the back- woods of America has set the world on fire."

Conditions were practically as bad as they had been during Queen Anne's War and the Deerfield Raid in 1704, when French led Indians wearing snowshoes trekked over three-hundred miles in the dead of winter and sneak attacked the Massachusetts settlement of Deerfield, late at night. Men were killed and scalped, buildings put to torch and women and children enslaved for ransom on the long march though snow and ice back to Canada. A savage had bashed a crying baby against a boulder, and other inhuman atrocities were committed. Fifty years later, terror still reigned across the frontier, where erection of French forts, and red-skin's scalping, blood-thirsty ambushes and murders continued.

Meanwhile, Pennsylvania's *Quakers* for 'brotherly love', and immigrant Germans from 'indifference' had refused to fight Indians. Other factions fabricated excuses, such as Massachusetts was a *Corporate Colony* and Virginia a *Crown Colony*. Unlike New France with one central government built upon the Beaver fur trade, each of the English settlements had different kinds of government and individual reasons for existence. Benjamin Franklyn suggested that the thirteen colonies unite to resolve their problems; but The British Crown disapproved of colonial indivisibility. Yet France must be expelled from Canada. And plans were being drawn up to capture *Louisburg* and other French bastions, including *Montreal* and even *Quebec City*. Britain and France were squaring off for a knock down, drag out fight – "Winner Take All!"

In the Lower Town of Quebec City, *Holy Child Chapel's* aisles overflowed with mourners. *Marie* had been popular. Grievers stood outside on the granite steps and in the narrow cobble-stone street leading to the funeral Mass, as buckets of rain poured down. Because Josef's masterpiece – *God the Benevolent Creator* – hung above the altar, his wife was to be honored with entombment in the crypt below the sanctuary. Otherwise only the most venerable priests and very wealthy people were buried there. Hundreds of beeswax candles had been lit to guide *Marie's* soul's upward journey into heaven.

Josef and Karen Bluejeans sat in the first pew. *Jacques-Pierre* sat beside her and next to his mother Joan. His father *Jacques-Louis*, Pena and Ortiz completed the row. Over her face Karen Bluejeans wore a black fishnet-veil of fine mesh given to her by *Madelaine de Repentigny*, the *Intendant's* mistress who lived near *White Owl's Nest* and had often gossiped to *Marie*. Mother Superior *Marie Etienne* sat behind the family. Each of the girls from school wore their uniform, a black chaplet, and a black ribbon tied with a pretty bow around their left arm. They sat together in front of the Ursuline Nuns. Together, they composed the choir that Sister *Marie Cecile* conducted while playing the old pipe-organ. *Annabelle*, an aristocratic child turned the music pages for the Nun. A song of consolation had been chosen from, *The Burgundy Hymnal For The Chapel Of French Kings. Michelle,* a profound beauty, vocalized solo soprano:

"I am the Resurrection, I am Life everlasting . ."

Marie's oak coffin decorated with white lilies had been laid out before the altar. The casque was closed because her body had turned as black as a Negro's, and it had swollen up into grotesque bulges. Father Greyrobe had not allowed Karen Bluejeans to see the corpse. Entrails had not been removed, as a necessity to the danger of contagion.

"Opening the box will disturb her final sleep. Let her rest in peace," he had told the young girl. "She has received *Extreme Unction*, Holy Mother the Church's last sacrament. She holds a Bible and a Rosary in her hands. She shall dwell in the everlasting joy of Paradise with our Lord. Her eyes, nose, ears and mouth need no adornments, cosmetics, spices or perfumes."

As the Solemn High Requiem Mass commenced, Karen Bluejeans remembered an earlier Spring when she was only three or four years old at Beaver Lodge. *Marie* had dressed her in a white dress and had placed a white flower behind her ear. The little girl had gathered up loose sticks and stray pieces of scrap wood and lined them up like a parade of wooden dolls or toy soldiers on the march. *Wolf* had helped carrying sticks to her in his mouth.

Picturesque against the fence post by the red barn from fallen seed had grown purple violets and dark green parsley amidst pale green weeds and goldenrod. A *Wood Turtle* about nine inches long and probably searching for a mate crawled through the vegetation. Along the fence rails the sun gleamed in a bright blue sky. The clear, slurred whistle of an *Eastern Meadowlark* sounded above the low, rattling chatter of *Wrens* and *Sparrows*. Her father threw back his head and laughed.

"What are you doing?" he cried, arms out raised in pretended surprise. Then he got serious.

"Karen Bluejeans, my daughter," he said. "Trees may have a spirit, but it is not the spirit of our people. Lay them out like this." The Woodcutter placed the sticks and pieces of wood straight forward horizontally, as they should rest before going into an oven's fire.

Marie's coffin was now situated in the same manner as the sticks. And the girl wondered if the spirit within the coffin-wood might present itself as a ghost? A ghost should look like one's breath on a frosty winter morning. She remembered a late February afternoon about two years ago, her family collecting maple syrup. Perfect conditions, the freezing night followed by a warm, thawing day. Pena had hitched up the donkeys like army mules to pull the sledge with the big tub. Buckets of maple sap fresh from the trees were emptied into this wooden container. Thirty-two gallons of sap boiled down to make one gallon of syrup. After a warm spell when buds appeared the trees could get tapped again; the sap would flow out like thick milk, then dribble a final few drops.

Mother had made a huge picnic lunch, cold slices of roast beef, apples-in-honey marmalade, sweet potatoes and 'turkey corn' [maize], pickled eels, wheat bread with pecan-nut spread, white-goose eggs hard boiled, and for dessert fresh fruit and anis-seed cakes, and sap spilled on the snow hardened into candy to suck on. We all drank spiced ale. Eskimo smoked a meerschaum pipe, the bowl carved to resemble a moose's head. His cherry tobacco smelled masculine. *Jacques-Pierre* started a snowball fight with Ortiz who looked like a little boy, "because there was no snow in ol' Mexico where he grew up," her mother explained. We were tired from the morning's hard work.

Then Pena with dark, sparkling eyes, pointed beard and long mustache like a catfish's arrived leading *Belle*. *Wolf* barked a welcome and everybody was revived. And the work went on for three more hours. He had stayed behind to take care of his honeybees and rare plants in the winter apiary and green-houses in the cellar of *Chanticleer*. They barely survived the cold weather. But once he was sure that they'd be okay he built two snowmen armed with broom handles for muskets to guard the gate at Beaver Lodge. Then he departed with the Musk Ox to join the maple syrup makers. He also brought a couple of feed-bags full of oats for '*Alec*' and *Heloise*, whom he fed and watered. Karen Bluejeans recalled that he had given her carrots to feed the Long-ears, while he placed blankets over the backs of the beasts of burden to keep them warm.

In her full length white Mink coat, *Marie* looked like the Ice Princess or *Freyja,* the *Norse* goddess of youth and love. She slowly twirled around and around as the big snowflakes about three-inches wide fell from the sky. Karen Bluejeans herself wore beaver-fur coat with hood, and knitted, multi-hued gloves, each finger was a different color. Imitating her mother she spun around and around beneath the large drifting snowflakes. She had wanted to wear the beaded Mic-Mak hat and mittens that *Pierre Noel* [Santa Claus] had left for her in the stocking she had hung on the fireplace mantle.

"No, darling!" her mother had said. "Save those clothes for Church."

Loving snow, *Wolf* had leaped up and down and barked. Like a lantern hanging in the sky, the glistening moon illuminated their return to the work-yard estate. Like a scout, *Wolf* led the party, followed by Karen Bluejeans atop *Belle,* the Musk Ox. *Jacques-Pierre* escorted them. The children sang, *Alouette* – "*Alouette, gentille Alouette, Alouette, je te plumerai. .*"

Walking the donkeys, Pena and Ortiz smoked Hemp, passing the cigar or joint between them, to not waste any of its euphoric-inducing substance. *Marie* held the reins and rode on the sledge with the spouts, empty buckets and full tub of maple sap. Eskimo walked along after her, jumping on and off the sledge and making small talk, sweet nothings into his wife's ear. Bells, on the sleigh's harness, jingle-jingle-jangled.

We had the loveliest of times, thought Karen Bluejeans.

Father Greyrobe turned around to the coffin before him and spoke:

"*Marie l' Arbre* was a devoted member of the Church, as well as a beloved wife and mother. She was our friend and good neighbor. She reflected the virtues of Canadian women: thrift, efficiency, common sense, industry and self-devotion to family. We bury her here at *Holy Child Chapel* that she will be close to our prayers."

Karen Bluejeans felt big tears sliding down her cheeks. She stifled a sob.

"We do not know why God chooses to take one person and not another," she heard the priest saying, "We can only believe that in His infinite wisdom He does what is best. *Marie* had a long life ahead of her, and yet the Lord called her to his side. She died suddenly. She did not suffer."

Whimpering, sobbing, crying sounds softly bounced, echoed and reverberated from the *Holy Child Chapel's* nooks and crannies.

"From now on, until the Last Judgment," said the priest with joy in his voice, "We may pray directly to *Marie* and ask her to intercede in heaven for us. She is next to Jesus, the Madonna, Angels, Saints and Holy Martyrs. She will help us to attain salvation." Waiving a golden censor, the priest made the air heavy with sweetly scented incense-smoke. He sang blessings and the remainder of the Mass.

Josef led the procession of people who filed past the deceased to pay their last respects. Upon a Medieval Harp, *Sister Marie Therese* played the *'Funeral Dirge'* from *Musica Sacra* [*Sacred Music*]. Behind the closely knit mesh of her black fishnet veil, Karen Bluejeans thanked each person in line. Silent and sullen *Red Feather* hugged her. Finally the coffin was lowered into an unadorned stone sarcophagus. Josef had in mind to later carve an appropriate epitaph.

"I await you and our rendezvous in Eden!"

"*Pluto* steals *Proserpine*!" muttered *Jacqueline*, a sophisticated older girl, to *Colette* and the twins. [*Pluto*, Pagan Rome's god of the Underworld, abducted the goddess of Spring-&-Summer to make her his bride. Without her the world experienced autumnal decay changing into a barren winter wasteland of snow; but just as her beauty melted the dark lord's icy heart and he permitted her to visit Mother Earth once a year, so does the cycle of seasons revolve yearly bringing the green buds of Spring followed by Summer.]

Karen Bluejeans did not go to *Monsieur La Roc's* restaurant where food and drink had been prepared for after the funeral. It was traditional in Canada to feed the mourners since many of them had to travel a long distance to attend a burial ceremony. Instead, she hurried back to *Wolf* at *White Owl's Nest*, – the gray skies promising further rain.

Jacques-Pierre did not walk her home. He stayed to drink

brandy with his father and the other men. She thought of him as she lit the candle on the shelf above her bed. There was his gift, the Holy Card of *Kateri Tekawitha*, – "the Lily of the Mohawks." Next to the picture was her mother's gift, a rag-doll with hair of yellow yarn. She took the doll to bed and cried herself to sleep like a little girl.

Wolf got up from the Polar Bearskin rug beside her bed when just before dawn Pena and Ortiz staggered home with a drunken Eskimo. Karen Bluejeans remained asleep. Later that morning she poured hot coffee for her father to drink as he sat at the kitchen table. Neither of them felt like talking, but finally she began:

"*Red Feather* has invited me to visit her village this summer."

"No," said Josef, rubbing his eyes with the palms of his hands. "You know that your mother didn't want you to go. You're too young."

"I must!" Karen Bluejeans, said. "I must learn to live like an Indian, too. Or else, I'll never know my true self."

"No," said Josef, again. "Your mother and I talked about this. And we decided that you could go to camp with *Red Feather* when you're twelve years old."

"Twelve!" she exclaimed, slamming her fist down onto the table like *Thor's* hammer, –

– a trait of her mother's. "That's not for another three years. What am I supposed to do in the meantime?"

"We discussed that also. I didn't want to tell you until your birthday, but things are different now that your mother has passed away; may the Lord bless her. I'll explain our plan." He hesitated and remembered *Marie* had worn her hair in one long, plaited braid that winter's day. She had looked beautiful in her blue apron and her back to the frost-flecked-filigree formed upon the windowpane. Snowfall had thickly blanketed Quebec City's steep roofs and narrow streets. Gently with forefinger and thumb he pinched his tears to prevent their slipping from his eyes. He cleared his throat. Karen Bluejeans now with arms folded, stood, her back against the China Cabinet, and listened.

"We thought that we could compromise until you visit *Red Feather's* village, *Above the Falls,* by purchasing you a pony. You could learn responsibility taking care of it."

"Oh, father," she said, "Yes!" She hugged him around his shoulders, as he sat at the table. "I'll treat him better than any pony in the world."

"Karen Bluejeans, you've all my love," he said softly. He didn't tell her that last night Joan had been asking about marrying her son to his daughter. Both families had vaguely scheduled the wedding for after the girl had experienced sixteen summers. *Jacques-Pierre* would be eighteen by then, old enough to provide for a wife and a family of their own. Since *Marie* died though, Joan sought that the children should marry sooner. She did not think it proper for an old man and a young girl to live together alone under one roof, –an adopted young girl, at that!

"We'll go to *Montreal* to get the pony when school lets out next week," he said.

"I love you father," she said and hugged him again.

With a population of around four-thousand people, *Montreal* was one-hundred miles southwest of Quebec City, by way of the St. Lawrence River. Only one highway, barely wide enough for an ox-cart, existed between the two cities. The river handled almost all traffic. In 1535, *Jacques Cartier* had visited the island that the Iroquois called, *Hochelaga.* To honor his sponsor, *King Francis I, Cartier* named the local mountain,

Mont Royal, from which the city derived its name, *Montreal.* Here shiny stones thought to be diamonds were only quartz, and the sobriquet, "*Canadian Diamond,*" indicating something that wasn't worth as much as one might think at first glance, came into being.

The three principal divisions of France's civilizing policy were built at *Montreal*: a military fort, the Church, and a trading post. The island city became the center of the French fur trade with Indians and trappers from the Great Lakes depositing thousands of beaver skins yearly. Farther up the river was the city of *Lachine*, named by the explorer *La Salle*, who thought that he had discovered the outskirts of *Mandarin China*. The quest to discover a Northwest Passage to the Orient had been France's primary goal in the New World. Christianizing the heathen Indians was only a secondary objective, initiated much by the writing in the Jesuit *Relations.* The Beaver fur trade followed as another secondary goal, though of greed.

A large trading depot was located near *Lachine* and there many different tribes of Indians kept representatives. White *Voyageurs* brought back furs and sold them for money. Usually the trappers had traded with the Indians deep within the interior of the forests for most of the furs.

Indians next brought other furs, and in return they received hatchets with steel heads and skinning knives, iron kettles, bolts of bright cloths, glass beads and trinkets, and sometimes firearms. People met from all over. The trading post store was enclosed in a fort-like stockade. A large cross thirty-feet high with the French Coat of Arms (*Fleur-de-Lis)* mounted on it had been erected on a small mound outside the gate. Indian lodges and Wig-Wams were established along separate alleys around the stockade. Near a corral on the settlement's edge, Indians from the central plains south of the Great

Lakes set their Tee-Pees. From these natives who hunted from horseback the innumerable American Bison or Buffalo, – Josef hoped for a pony.

Cheyenne Indians of the Great Plains did have a yearling horse-pony for Karen Bluejeans. White with chestnut-brown spots, and bluish-black stockings, mane and tail, – the pony measured fourteen hands (fifty-nine inches) at the shoulder, almost qualifying as a full grown horse, which Pena had instructed Josef to look for. Also, the advice of *Jacques-Louis* was followed by providing plenty of brandy for the Indians to drink during the negotiations.

The pony appeared strong and healthy. Canada had no horses until *King Louis XIV* sent, as gifts, four stallions and forty-four mares, between 1665-1670; but not all of them survived the rigorous Atlantic Ocean crossing.

"I'm sure this animal is not a Canadian diamond," Eskimo said to his daughter.

"I'm going to call him *Paint*," she said stroking the noble equine creature's back. She winked and danced around him singing: "Poney and rider are one!"

Eohippus, the Dawn Horse, only as big as a dog or a small goat, originated around 50,000,000 years ago, dwelling in the Near East's *Fertile Crescent*, between *the Tigris* and *the Euphrates Rivers*, or in Persia. He sojourned there from the steppes of Central Asia, the same ground traversed (in 451 A.D.) by shaggy Mongolian horse-ponies carrying the barbaric hordes of *Attila the Hun*, 'the Scourge of God', and the greatest horseman the earth has ever seen.

In 1492, Spain's *King Ferdinand V of Aragon* and *Queen Isabella of Castile* financed Genoese navigator Christophe Columbus with the flagship *Santa Maria*, and escort ships *Pinto* and *Nina* to prove that the world was round by sailing

into the West towards his destination of China and the ex-
otic lands in the East. But instead of landing on *the Japanese
Islands* and collecting the riches of the Orient, he discovered
naked brown natives, green parrots and orange yams on the
Bahamas Island of *San Salvador*. Nevertheless, he has gotten
credit for discovering the New World that *Amerigo Vespucci* a
map-maker from Italy later named *America*. On the Admiral's
second voyage, Columbus took horses.

And in 1519, Conquistador, *Hernando de Cortes* introduced the war horse to conquer the Mesoamerican Empire of
Emperor Montezuma. His broad sword, tempered with blood
in the flames of holy Toledo's steel mills, bore the inscription:
"To Holy Mary, Mother of God, Christ, Jesus!" *Huitzilopochtli*
(Aztec War God) sobbing, fled, dripping blood from his
wounds and dragging his entrails in the dirt like raw meat for
the dogs! Eventually, some Spanish horses escaped and pop-
ulated the Far West, where the Cheyenne procured the *Pinto*
Pony that Karen Bluejeans had decided to name *Paint*.

❦

En Route to *Fort Duquesne* (near the site of present day
Pittsburg) British General Braddock, surprised by French
directed Indians, died in battle. Before his adjutant George
Washington buried him in an anonymous grave dug in the
road to prevent desecration of the dead, he offered two state-
ments: "We shall better know how to deal with them another
time;" and, "Who would have thought it?"

Both Braddock and Washington had had several horses
shot out from under them. It was a major defeat for the
English, and more tough luck for young American volunteer,
Indian fighter Mark Cronath. The vanquishment signaled that

the British mode of European warfare could not effectively compete with the guerilla tactics of the French Canadians and their Indians allies. Washington retired to Mount Vernon, his estate for the rest of the war.

CHAPTER IV.

Summer vacation started yesterday. And today, thirteen-years-old, Karen Bluejeans rode *Paint*, her pony, bareback away from Beaver Lodge in Quebec City's backyard, and headed northwest towards the Christian Indian village, *Above the Falls*. *Red Feather* sat behind Karen Bluejeans with her arms around the waist of the older girl. *Wolf* ran alongside of them, some times procrastinating rearward and other times venturing ahead.

Josef had given her money to pay some villagers to feed *Wolf* and *Paint*. This was his daughter's opportunity to learn Indian ways. *Monsieur Jourdain*, a retired French cavalry officer had taught her the basics of riding, which she had been performing, as well as taking care of the pony, for almost three years. Of course, Pena, as chief hostler had helped her. He had fed and groomed the animal on a daily basis. She mainly exercised and brushed the steed who was well liked in the barn. *Belle,* the Musk Ox and the donkeys were his friends. *Wolf,* too.

Pena gave her explicit instructions about caring for *Paint* during the summer at the Huron village. He also handed her a magic medicine of white powder called cocaine. Wrapped in a wad of cocoa leaves, the crushed dust hid in the medicine pouch that she could wear around her neck.

"Eat it!" he said. "You'll get superhuman powers of endurance for several days."

She nodded in understanding.

"Save a little of it and smoke that. You'll feel its strength within a minute or two. Smoking goes straight to the brain," he explained. A little pipe carved like a bird, with a small bowl and a tiny stem to inhale the burning substance, fit into the pouch. "Cocaine's effect takes longer to sense when you eat. That's because the powder must get digested into your blood stream."

"So it's best to eat cocaine for stamina, and then to smoke cocaine a little for an immediate effect?" she asked.

"Yes," said, Pena. "Remember, use it only for an emergency. Cocaine is addicting. Your body can become a slave to it, if taken too often."

"I shall not forget, my friend," said, Karen Bluejeans, placing her right hand on Pena's left shoulder, as an indication of acceptance. She tied the leather laces of the purse around her neck. Woodland Indians frequently wore such a bag filled with herbs and other healing remedy.

She didn't notice it again while riding *Paint* in a leisurely manner with *Red Feather*. They had almost reached the bridge that stretched over the steep drop to the river's rapids water below.

"After we cross the bridge you'll come to a fork," whispered the village Chief's daughter, into the ear of Karen Bluejeans. "The far road after the bridge goes to *Montreal*. That path to the right takes us past the waterfalls to my village." They rode towards the rickety bridge, which had a railing only on its northern side, while upstream the water came crashing down in a thunderous roaring that almost deafened the vacation bound students.

Karen Bluejeans turned to her rider and said, "This bridge is structurally dangerous!"

And then it happened so fast that neither of the girls were sure of what was actually happening. *Paint* reared up on his hind legs. *Red Feather* fell off the horse immediately and slammed into the bridge's feeble railing. A big cat like a *Western Mountain Lion* leaped from the other side of the gap and swiped a big claw at *Paint's* head. The pony had detected the cat's scent seconds before the attack. The equid had dodged death, but his neck was ripped and bleeding. Karen Bluejeans was trying to reassure him and also hanging on desperately to not fall off his back.

Paint reared up again. Karen Bluejeans used her legs to make the big pony back away from the bridge. The panther-like beast had lost balance momentarily during the lunge and almost fell off the bridge to certain death. Within less than a minute the attacker squared his shoulders and blocked the bridge like some troll from a fairytale. *Red Feather* froze against the rail, prepared to die. Then *Wolf* rushed forth and launched himself against the forest tiger. Theirs was blood-red! Tooth and nail and claw, – "Survival of the Fittest!"

Everything continued to take place very fast. The total scene could not be witnessed. Quickly dismounting, Karen Bluejeans slipped *Paint's* reins around a shrub. Next, she grabbed *Red Feather's* shirt collar and dragged the stunned child away from bridge and animal combat. Eskimo had taught his daughter how to load and shoot a musket, but nobody thought of arming her with a firearm just to ride out to *Above the Falls*. Suddenly she recalled the knife Ortiz had strapped to her boot.

She unsheathed the blade and straddled her side of the bridge. Her left hand wiped her long disarrayed hair from her face. Her right hand gripped the knife ready to deliver an uppercut. Like a prehistoric cave-woman figure she crouched, baring her teeth. But her reinforcement, had not arrived soon enough.

Profusely bleeding from *Wolf's* bites, the seriously wounded feline slunk away. The dog sprawled motionless on the bridge in a heap of bloody bones and slashed pieces of fur. *Red Feather* screamed hysterically. She kept turning around in circles, both hands covering her ears, and screaming! In the background *Paint* was trying to rear up, tugging and pulling to get loose from the shrub where his mistress had tied him. He emitted panicking noises.

Karen Bluejeans stumbled onward. Feeling faint and dizzy she grasped onto the bridge rail and took a series of deep breaths. With the increased oxygen she comprehended that *Wolf* was dead, but she couldn't mourn for him at this moment. They had to get out of the area. The lion might return. What to do first? She ran over to *Red Feather* and seized and shook the shoulders of the Huron Princess.

"Quiet down!" she shouted. She pulled the younger one's hands away from the ears and put them around her own neck. Then she hugged and squeezed the girl, pleading into her ear: "Please show courage. We've got to focus. *Red Feather, Red Feather* act strong!"

Sobbing, *Red Feather* stood up straight, tears cascading down her cheeks. Karen Bluejeans comforted her by patting a hand upon the smaller girl's back, as though burping a baby. "Wait with *Paint*. Calm him down," she said. Next, she ran to *Wolf.*

She too now began to cry. Kneeling down and scraping

up his body, her breasts heaving with convulsions. His lifeless head rested on her shoulder as she carried his remains to the pony. *Red Feather* opened her bundle of clothes and offered her uniform jumper to wrap *Wolf*. Her blouse already served as a bandage for *Paint*, his neck glassy with blood. Karen Bluejeans administered First Aid, soaked up blood and pressure-stopped the bleeding with clothes she had packed for camp. She put *Wolf* on *Paint's* back and led them towards Beaver Lodge. *Red Feather* clung to the older girl's arm. The cougar didn't menace them again.

Wolf was buried on the mound under the Cherry Tree just before the little apple orchard. He had enjoyed resting there with his ball or a chew bone and watching events in the work-yard. His ball was put into the grave with him. Eskimo had wrapped him in the Polar Bear skin that he had slept on even before Karen Bluejeans had come to *White Owl's Nest*. Ortiz buried the water bowl and food dish of their beloved comrade with him that he should have a nice home in the next world. Overnight Josef engraved a tombstone commemorating the smiling Huskie's face, name and epitaph:

WOLF – "May earth's dust weigh not hard against me."

Father Greyrobe blessed the funeral. He had thought that he might mention Jesus, the Good Shepherd who loved the lost lamb, as an example of kindness to animals. *Wolf* though had been a wolf and not a lamb so the parable didn't seem to fit in. Instead the priest talked about Saint Francis and God's love of all creatures.

Karen Bluejeans maintained a solemn mood throughout the service. She had already sobbed her heart out. Now she only desired that *Wolf* have rest in peace. Her mother should take care of him in heaven just as she had cared for him in Quebec City.

Red Feather, though upset at *Wolf's* death and burying, was anxious to return home to the Huron Village, *Above the Falls.* After a practical discussion, the family at Beaver Lodge felt that Karen Bluejeans should go on to the Mission Indian village to camp for the summer as planned.

Algonquian, Abenaki Mic-Mak ("The People") had prepared the baby girl, whom Josef had found almost thirteen year earlier. Although the *Huron* ("Dwellers of the Peninsula") were *Iroquoian* farmers, they should prove true enough to her quest for Native American identity. Eskimo set forth the rationale:

"You can't die with *Wolf* any more than you could die with your mother. You must go on living. Let them live through you. Stay true to yourself, as they'd have wanted you to do."

Jacques-Pierre escorted the girls, armed with musket, pistol, sword, hatchet and knife. Neither wild animals nor anything else should get in their way. He rode *Helena* and Karen Bluejeans and *Red Feather* rode ol' *Alec.* The sure-footed donkeys substituted for *Paint,* while the equine survivor of the feline attack convalesced.

The girls were forty-eight hours behind their schedule; hence, nobody indicated surprise when scouts from the village met them soon after they had crossed the bridge. Camp had wondered what happened to their girl and her guest. One of the boys, *Rain Cloud,* helped *Red Feather* jump off the donkey and they embraced. They kissed in the French fashion with tongues.

"I will never separate from you again," she said breathlessly, and wept on his shoulder.

Karen Bluejeans dismounted too. She hugged *Jacques-Pierre* and kissed him good-bye. He stayed at the bridge until her party was not visible. He looked around. The terrain was rough and rocky. The appearance of the huge heavy cat here had been a rarity. This was the land of the Canada Lynx [*Lynx Canadensis*]. At most a lynx didn't weigh more than seventy pounds.

"*Karen Bluejeans*, please take care for all of us," said the French-Canadian youth. And then he rode away leading *Alexander* behind the Jenny, as easily as if she were a dangling carrot.

Golden Bear, a teenage warrior who would someday be Chief, and *Rain Cloud*, the boy whom *Red Feather* loved, took the girls safely to the village hidden in the forest, *Above the Falls*.

"The puma must die as punishment for scaring *Red Feather*," said *Rain Cloud*, sternly, with the awareness of some-body living in the stone-age.

"I will hunt down and kill the panther," *Golden Bear* told Karen Bluejeans. "I'll avenge your brave *Wolf*." He found fragments of two days old tracks and other markings. He followed them to a cave, where two big lion cubs were dozing, waiting for their mother to return with food. The cubs were undoubtedly the cause of the cat's head on attack of *Paint*. In Africa the khaki-colored Lioness leaps upon a black-&-white striped *Zebra* from behind, just as India's orange *Bengal Tiger*, burning bright, pounces upon an enormous elephant's back. This mother's direct assault tactics had been motivated by desperation for food to feed her little ones.

Without discussion *Rain Cloud* ran forth and brained both cubs with a heavy, water-worn- pebble tomahawk. He quickly slit the throats of the stunned animals, and hung them up at the entrance of the cave. *Golden Bear* grunted approval, and beneath the dead babies, opened wide the metal jaws of a fur trapper's trap. Leaves concealed the mechanism's sharp teeth. The Indians hid and waited for the carnivorous creature. She arrived limping home with a dead raccoon in her mouth. Maternal instinct sympathized with the dead infants. She dropped their dinner and burst forth towards her cubs.

"Snap!" The trap sprang shut. The clamping force tore deeply into the lion's right foreleg. With a whoop, *Golden Bear* moved in for the kill and shot several arrows into the animal. Normally he might have let the cat slowly bleed out to death. Sitting near to the suffering beast he would have made a thanksgiving prayer for its spirit. But he hadn't any time for that now. Excitedly, *Golden Bear* sought the company of Karen Bluejeans.

Later he gave her the lioness skin to wear as a hooded cloak. Cunning, swiftness and other powers went with the individual who wore the garment. Karen Bluejeans chose *the Cougar* for her *Manitou* (supernatural psyche) to guide her. She had been planning to choose *the Porcupine*, because she liked the quiet, reflective path-finding qualities associated with the sharp bristled character. Their quills colored with vegetable dyes were woven into belts, leggings, blouses, boxes and trunks, jewelry, purses and bags for medicine or tobacco. Quillwork business blended in with her merchant-like family. And more than once the Porcupine had saved Woodland Mic-Mak lives, since it was easy to catch, especially in between Summer's food (fish, crustaceans, mollusks, nuts & plants) and cold Winter's deep snows that helped capture *Caribou* and *Moose*. They were not farmers like the Huron. Written white accounts described the Porcupine as tasting like wild pig. And once when playing with *Wolf* along the cliff edges of *the City*, she had met a family of Hedgehog-like inhabitants in their den. Now things had changed. Porcupine was too tame. *Golden Bear's* cougar was tougher. All summer long the young Huron taught her the ways of the Indian.

He instructed her in the savage techniques for making and using Bow-&-Arrows, Tomahawk and Scalping Knife. And they wrestled, Indian style. She learned some strong throws. One afternoon while practicing, he flung her down in the luxuriant green grass and fell on top of her. Her face felt hot and her dark brown eyes emanated sultriness. *Golden Bear* tried to kiss the maiden beneath him. She resisted. He rolled over onto his back. Then to his astonishment she rolled over on top of him. They kissed and were one person together. From the corner of her eye Karen Bluejeans witnessed a Blue Jay (a member of the Crow set) flash in the dappled sunlight like cascading shiny silver coins.

At that time, sailing out of *the English Channel* from Portsmouth, Admiral Boscawen commanded the British invasion fleet; twenty-two Ships of the Line and many smaller vessels departed for France's Gibraltar of the New World, *Louisburg*, at the mouth of the St. Lawrence. The French Navy itself was actually bottled up in the Mediterranean Sea or in *Brest* in *Brittany*.

ENGLAND RULES THE WAVES!

Due to 'Gravel' (an intestinal malady) and 'Rheumatism' (from exposure during Winter), Wolfe was nervous, irritable and seasick aboard the convoy's flagship. He wrote: "There perhaps has never been a more extraordinary voyage. The continual opposition of contrary winds, calms, or current baffled all our skill and wore out all our patience." Some sailors had begun to call the tall, lanky soldier, with red hair like a fox, – "the passenger."

"Navigation on the river itself is a problem," continued Wolfe. "1711, Admiral Hovenden Walker lost half his fleet to squalls off the North Coast in the Gulf of the St. Lawrence. He was forced to return home empty-handed.

The *Quebecois* believed the victory was won through prayers for the Divine Intercession of the Virgin *Marie*." (Josef had implored the Virgin for aid and to help him transport the papoose he had taken back to *the City*, promising to carve the Madonna a *DeVoto* statue for *Holy Child Chapel*, which he did produce).

"Tempests enormously contributed to the destruction of the so-called *Invincible Spanish Armada*, in 1588," said Jack. "And earlier just before Marco Polo's visit, in 1274, China's mighty *Emperor Kublai Khan* sent 900 ships and 40,000 men to take over the island kingdom of Japan. A typhoon devastated the Chinese invasion fleet. All was lost to a high and holy wind: '*the Kamikaze*', sent by *Amatera o Mikami* (sun goddess) and *Susano o No* (storm god), protectors of *the Japanese Islands*."

"Not any foreign gods will obstruct my taking *Louisburg* or Quebec City," replied Wolfe, placing the Elephant-&-Castle Rook onto the chart of the St. Lawrence waterway that they had been regarding. The troubled Atlantic Ocean storm-tossed the massive British flotilla.

At Halifax, Bosun Billy 'Boy' Jones awaited the arrival of Jack Wales and Britain's invasion fleet. Most of his free time was spent listening to Shannon Yardley, a young Scandinavian-blonde woman, sing at the Tavern, *St. George & the Dragon*. A painted sign hanging above the door illustrated Saint George as England's *Red Cross Knight* riding a white horse and slaying with lance the dark-green, black-winged *Dragon of Evil*.

Early one evening the Bosun observed a huge muscular Negro win an arm-wrestling match. Bets had been made and there was lots of action collecting and paying money. There were no follow up challengers. Billy bought the bloke a beer.

"Thanks," said the black man. "Puttin' down the next strong man works up a mighty thirst."

Billy explained that he was expecting the British fleet sent to capture *Louisburg*. They talked and by the end of the night the black man had agreed to sign on as Jack's Orderly. His name was Able Freeman. And this is his story.

In Boston Massachusetts, the Pastor Reverend Woolen Mather bought and freed *Jove,* the black slave from Virginia. With freedom came the name Abel Freeman. Since he had been trained like his father as a blacksmith, he easily found work aboard a Whale-Hunter, as the ship's armorer-mechanic, making and maintaining metal devices for sailing, including but not limited to nails, hooks, harpoons, anchors, winches, and other tools, weapons and varied implements. But he had missed the boat, and he had been left stranded when Billy Boy had convinced the big man that working in the British Navy as Jack's man should be worth the time and effort.

The good-looking, blond Bosun closed his pitch: "When *Boreas*, the North Wind blows, you'll weather storms well, a seaman in King George's Navy. All Bristol & Sterling."

Abel's own sire had been beaten up, captured and traded by *the Ashanti* tribe to Portuguese Slavers off the coast of West Africa. The captive native survived an inhuman ocean voyage to be manacled and sold on the auction block at *Hampton Roads* near Norfolk Virginia. Following Spanish examples of slave labor for sugar fields in the *West Indies* and gold mines in *South America*, the English tobacco plantations had sought slaves since 1700.

Massachusetts had condoned slavery since 1624. Negroes were traded with salt, cotton and tobacco. Experience had taught that a New England white man worked better than three or four black men, but one Black was worth half a dozen or more red men. Indians captured and sold as slaves for sugar plantations on *Saint-Dominique (Haiti), Hispaniola*, and *Martinique* simply died. Unlike a Black Boy, the Red Man was not born for Slavery's Yoke. The South religiously practiced that the Negro Race descended from the posterity of Noah's son, *Ham,* who (after the Flood & Rainbow) had seen his father drunk and naked. For punishment *Ham's* progeny was condemned to serve as slaves. Such bondage was justified in *the Holy Bible, 1611 Edition, King James Version – the Booke of Genesis; Chapter IX., Verses 20-25.*

Billy and Abel got up to leave since the sailor had promised the Black a place to sleep. Just as they got to the door the girl who had sung called attention to herself. She and Billy were physically attracted to one another. Performing with the guitar, a popular, relatively new bedroom instrument from *Castile,* she strummed the strings-strung sound box and sang her song, which was written by King Henry VIII, – *Greensleeves:*

"Alas my love you do me wrong, to treat me thus so discourteously,

For I have loved thee so long, delighting in thy company. ."

Bluejacket Billy gave her one last, long, wistful look, as he adjusted his round sailor-hat.

While aboard Admiral Boscawen's flagship *Princess Amelia,* General Wolfe and Jack regarded a large, spread map of Quebec to apprehend the possibility of attacking *the City* before returning to England.

"We don't want to count our chickens before they've hatched," Wales said; "but *Louisburg* will capitulate." In the back of his mind Wolfe was thinking of his sweetheart, Catherine Lowther, later called Kate (or the Duchess). If the young General could take Quebec City and get back home before Winter's ice crystals froze into the St. Lawrence River, then Wolfe would marry the voluptuous 'Bride-To-Be' in Olde London Town during Christmastide.

"Capturing Quebec City will cause the strangulation of Canada," he said. The Canadian cannot escape our choking throat hold; nor shall supplies from France succor him."

"The Kirkes did that, in 1629. They starved *Samuel Champlain* into submission," said Jack.

"The gist of my plan is to land east of *the City* and to maneuver around back to the West Side, where the land is higher. From that position we can shoot down into the Upper Town," James explained.

"That was Sir William Phipp's plan in 1690; wasn't it?" Jack asked.

"It was. Quebec denied Phipps possession, because he didn't get across *the St. Charles River* on the East Side," said Wolfe.

"*Governor, Louis de Buade, Comte de Frontenac* made a big name for himself by refusing to give up against a superior force," said Jack. "He said something like: 'Let the mouth of my cannon answer your ultimatum to surrender.'"

"Phipps had to withdraw because he couldn't risk freezing the fleet in the frozen water of the approaching Winter," said Wolfe, his eyebrows heavy with emphasis. "That's what we must avoid too. We won't have time to starve them. The river will freeze first. The Royal Navy can't take the chance of allowing its ship to break up in the ice; also the stuck vessels should prove vulnerable targets to ground attacks by the French and their Indian allies.

"Why don't we just land on the West Side, as the Kirke Brothers did around sixty years earlier than Phipps?" said Jack, as he placed upon the map an Elephant-&-Castle Rook. James did note the location of the piece, *the Plain of Abraham.*

The Union Jack flew over Quebec City for several years," agreed Wolfe, "but it was traded through peace negotiations.

And an underlying problem was that the British Navy was unable to defend the place at that time. The Navy is another factor. Lack of cooperation between the services cost us defeat at *Rochefort* along the Atlantic coast of France. However, there are several reason why we cannot attack directly on the West Side of *the City*. The safest landing spot is twenty miles away towards *Montreal* at *Cap Rouge*. Steep cliffs prevent a closer landing. As we march eastward to the walls of Quebec City we risk getting caught in between its army and the French-Canadian Army of the West, our backs against the cliff edge with a three-hundred foot drop to the St. Lawrence River."

The river's wind welcomed Karen Bluejeans.

Early every morning she had awoken to the songs of birds declaring their territory from tree branches, bushes and forest under-story: 'the sweet, musical zip' of the *Magnolia Warbler*; 'the buzz' of the *Black-throated Warbler*; 'the high, thin teee tee tee' of the *Bay-breasted Warbler*; and other birds, such as the *Thrush, Linnet* and *Lark* ascending, – 'their whistle, call and chirrup'. She learned Squaw ways: how to choose young saplings to make a Wig-Wam; how to build a fire and how to cook; how to sew clothes and string beads; and other arts and crafts native to the American Indian Woman.

Soon before harvest festival, at summer's end, Karen Bluejeans and *Red Feather* went hunting for *Grey Partridge*. They heard the low hooting of a *Spruce Grouse*. The younger girl abruptly halted and pointed to the bird she was named after, a *Northern Cardinal*.

"I'm pregnant! I won't go back to school," she said in sign language. Then swaying her hips from side to side, she giggled: "Tell Mother Superior that I'll not be taking the veil." The startled birds flew away.

Rain Cloud and *Red Feather* were married. For the

ceremony, she wore knee-high, wedding-dance boots fabricated from the lion's cubs. The head of a young cat peered at the toe of each boot, and a tail hung from behind the knee-high cuffs. There was much food, dancing, singing and man feats of skill. A contest featuring long sticks (reminiscent of a Bishop's Crosier or Abbot's Crozier) curved at one end for a webbing of catgut to keep ball control, was played. Later this sport became Canada's national game: *La Crosse!* Karen Bluejeans gave the eleven-year-old bride a silver necklace as her wedding gift.

After the all-night partying, *Golden Bear* walked the Mic-Mak teenager to the bridge, in the pre-dawn darkness. He wore a leather loincloth, and his hair was bristly, like a "boar's head,' the traditional Huron style. His silent tongue inadequately substituted for all that he yearned to say to his beautiful friend. They could hear the rapids-running, river water roaring far below. She presented him a silver-handled pistol for a farewell present. Then Karen Bluejeans kissed his cheeks, and said: *"Adieu, mon cher."*

A crack of dawn severed the Eastern horizon. The wind whispered entreaties through the branches of trees. Seven honking geese flew overhead in V-formation. And Karen Bluejeans recalled that in the Mic-Mak myth *Canada Goose* honks as prayer for flight guidance from *Glooskap* the creator. She could smell the St. Lawrence's scents as she sauntered into Beaver Lodge just before high noon. She adorned a beaded fly-mask upon the pretty pony, *Paint,* who was recovering well because of Pena's care. She smiled bravely.

"Lord Jaguar did not triumph over us," he said, observing the teen and her pony.

After washing the grime and sweat of the road from her body, she perfumed herself and visited *Wolf.* She laid the cougar-skin cape over his grave: "Now you have all of her strength," she said. A single tear of grief fell from the girl's eye, and then a stream of sorrow.

At Halifax, Wolfe's anger over lack of discipline prevailed. He complained:

"Portsmouth was an infernal den full of dirty, drunken, insolent rascals. Every kind of corruption, immorality and looseness was carried to excess. But Halifax is absurd. Too much money and too much rum. Sergeants drunk on duty and the rest of the army wallowing in the dirt." He was glad when Jeffrey Amherst (the supreme commander of the invasion force) gave 'the go ahead' to the new Brigadiers: Lawrence, Whitmore and himself, the future Deliverer, at the birth of the British Empire, – James Wolfe.

June 02, 1758. Over 150 sail with 12,000 troops rode out the rough seas west of *Louisburg* for a week. Wolfe's brigade hit the beach at *Freshwater Cove.* Several boats crushed, many Englishmen drown in the high surf and Wolfe signaled a return to the ships that was misunderstood. Jack, Billy and Abel rushed ashore with the very first boatload. Wolfe, 'for Army-Navy co-operation reasons', had ridden in another boat. (While in the Far East, Jack had purchased a mahogany cane from the rain-forest jungles of *Macau*, a Portuguese colony along the coast of Southeast China. When Wolfe admired the thin, lacquered, walking stick. Jack immediately gave it to him). The General now up-raised the cane as he leaped into the surging water and led the foremost troops. Behind him came the *Light Infantry* (grenadiers and marksmen), *American Rangers, Fraser's Highlanders* and more companies of grenadiers. They stormed the French coastal defense battery with bayonet. British artillery was landed.

Louisburg's defenses began to crumble. Under the heavy

siege bombardment the fortress collapsed after 51 days of resistance. The French navy could not provide assistance because of the enormous British fleet's presence. No tempests interfered, nor Acts of God. Sickness didn't strike down the English; and there wasn't any quibbling between the Services, as during the abortive raid at *Rochefort* (where Wolfe's tactical brilliance first flashed before Prime Minister William Pitt's ken). *Marquis de Montcalm's* reserve forces were fighting about the "lakes route," to *Montreal* and could not be spared to rescue the French fortress. The *Coup De Grace* (or death stroke) was actually conceived by Jack, and because of it he'd receive consideration for Knighthood.

The daring scheme was promoted through Wolfe to General Amherst and Admiral Boscawen. Late at night, the Royal Marine Major captained six hundred sailors who silently rowed into the harbor and captured the last French Ship of Line. France's *General Drucor* surrendered. British General Amherst received: eleven stands of Colours, almost 6,000 prisoners, more than 200 cannon and mortars, over 14,000 stands of arms and shot, thousands of barrels of gunpowder and many supplies. Brave Wolfe was singled out as Victorious Hero.

"Quebec City is impregnable!" officially proclaimed *Governor Vaudreuil. Louisburg* had been lost, but French morale was high. To celebrate Quebec's invincibility, *the Governor* was throwing a Ball!

Karen Bluejeans knew all about the big dance. Wearing a plaid woolen skirt, a blue denim shirt and a fringed leather-jacket, she waited for *Jacques-Pierre* at the entrance of Beaver Lodge, the stone house *Chanticleer* on one side, the little windmill to saw logs off away on the other side. She could see him. He picked up his pace and they embraced and kissed. For her old boyfriend her mouth was full of honey to sweeten the taste of her kiss. Inside the work yard from the dove-cote above the gate, mourning doves were cooing coo woo rooing.

"Some of the girls from school are going to help serve refreshments at *the Governor's Ball*. Eskimo is in charge of the firewood and all the candles. You can supervise the part-time helpers. *RSVP*," she said breathlessly.

"Count me in," he said, wiping his mouth on the sleeve of his shirt. "But listen, little one. The Latin Club at Seminary School is going to join up with the militia. We're going to have our own unit, – *The Blue Musketeers of the Blessed Virgin!* Blue is Mary's color. I'll be in charge. It's a step to becoming governor: '*Veni, Vidi, Vici!*'"

She recognized the Latin, Julius Caesar's words uttered upon crossing the Rubicon, before becoming virtual dictator of Rome: "I came, I saw, I conquered." Nevertheless, when wasn't *Jacques-Pierre* pretentious?

"Oh, *Jacques-Pierre!*" she said, smiling, her cream-colored lipstick looking wet and glossy:

"You'll look handsome in a military uniform." He had grown an inch taller than she, who now put her arms up around his neck. Pale green leaves wavered above them in the background.

Thanks to *The Blue Musketeers* and others, Karen Bluejeans believed that *the City* was safe for the time being. *The Governor's* propaganda efforts had proven effective. And although Wolfe was acknowledged as the Hero of *Louisburg*, Amherst refused any attempt at taking Quebec City. It was too late in the year. They could not hazard becoming stranded in Canada's frozen Winter. Instead Wolfe received orders to police around the Gulf of St. Lawrence, to put the fear of the Lord into the fishing villages and rural farms.

His proclamation promising friendship was answered by

only a group of about twenty-five Christian Indians, widows, children and a few old grandpas. On their way to the British outpost a French regiment intercepted them. The officer in charge, acting on his own self-initiative, shepherded the Indians, like a flock of goats, into a natural ditch. His soldiers were commanded to shoot the savage traitors. A corporal questioned the order.

"Sir!" he said. "Won't we waste our musket balls?"

"Waste them!" replied his superior.

Soon after a scouting party of American Rangers, with smirking, Indian fighter Mark Cronath, whose father had been slaughtered by savages many years ago, found the open mass-grave of dead, scalped bodies. Wolfe wrote home: "I cannot look coolly upon these hell-hounds."

He returned to England, unaware that orders had been sent to him. Ships had passed in the night. Nonetheless, Jack Wales and his crew, Billy "Boy" Jones and Able Freeman had already received the General's permission to reconnoiter the St. Lawrence before ice blocked waterway passage.

"I don't know if we'll be able to see anything with all this fog and mists," said Billy, steady at the tiller. Sword and pistol at his feet, Jack held the telescope up to his eye ready to catch a glimpse of the shore the moment the weather should break. Under an oily brown, Mariner's Jacket he wore his Redcoat. "We want this thick pea soup," he said, softly. "It keeps us hidden from the *Frog*." ["*Frog*," slurred the French who enjoyed the gourmet delicacy of frog legs.]

"Hee hee," chuckled, big Abel. His strong white teeth animated his black face. He sat in the bow of the boat holding a harpoon and controlling the Jib Sail. Jack's use of the English language had amused him. Boldly he spoke: "Ol' Toady got too many peas in his soup to see what's happening."

"Sshhh!" whispered Billy. He thought that he had heard something rippling in the water.

But it was too late. Their conversation had given them away. Within less than a second, a large canoe full of over twenty Indian warriors quietly pulled alongside the little sailboat. Another canoe came out of the dense cloud on their other side. The enemy wore green and gray paints that blended into the water and atmosphere. Jack sitting amidships tried to dive under the boom and to pull up his pistol. As fast as a shark, an Indian clubbed him on the head with a gnarled-ball tomahawk, conking Jack out.

A navy of decorated, birch-bark war canoes, fifty or more, suddenly emerged from the pale fog. Abel was subdued by threat of several arrows aimed at him from multiple directions. He couldn't assist the Major. Still the savages remained silent.

Only when one rude red fellow loudly yelped, as he slipped a leather leash around Billy's neck did their hideous whooping begin. A maniac noise chorus echoed and re-echoed over the opaque, aqueous channel. They had gotten a big prize, they had overwhelmed a Spy Boat!

Chef Beuf, the greasy Frenchman in charge of canoe patrol, told *Jacques-Louis* to take Jack as prisoner for presentation to the *Marquis de Montcalm* and *Vaudreuil* himself. Because he was black like the devil, Abel was put to Bishop *Levele.* But the tall, bald-headed Indian who had collared Billy had already taken the Bosun away. After running the gauntlet (a pathway between two rows of brute warriors, and this time some tribal women and children armed with clubs, rocks and straps, the prisoner was coerced to run while suffering blows and whippings), Jones would be tortured, especially by the women and children, who resented his white skin and blond hair. Then he'd be cooked and eaten alive.

Jacques-Louis reported the capture immediately upon returning to Quebec City. *Marquis de Montcalm, Francois Bigot* (the *Intendant)*, and Joe *Cadet* (his dishonest assistant) attending the Ball, delayed their departure until the chamber Orchestra had begun to play a *Minuet*. Like many other women present, Karen Bluejeans's coiffure was the bouffant, white-powdered wig favored at *Versailles. Madelaine de Repentigny* (the *Intendant's* mistress and a friend of *Marie*, the Mic-Mak girl's mother), had dressed up Karen Bluejeans to appear much more provocative than a maiden of a mere thirteen or fourteen years. While the lines of dancers moved, the gang of authorities slipped away to the garrison guard rooms where Jack was held in custody. He sat upon a wooden bench, his hands tied behind his back.

Montcalm talked with him for a few moments, and then tuned to *Bigot*.

"Keep this rascal unharmed," he ordered. "We might use him for prisoner exchange." *The Marquis* avoided returning to the Ballroom, and instead went back to his own quarters.

Sneering at Jack, the *Intendant* theatrically called out: "Cast him into the dungeon!"

Then he walked over to the next room and kicked Abel in the head. *Cadet*, following close behind like a Rear Guard, burst out laughing. "This nigger won't start insurrection here," said the *Intendant,* breathing heavily because of the exertion involved with his kick. Although, slavery had been legal in Canada since 1709, it had never been very productive. *Bigot* ordered a squad of policemen. "Take him away and whip his black back red with blood!"

Bishop *Levele* suddenly approached. He and the *Intendant* had disagreed and argued many times before, therefore *Bigot* glared suspiciously at the Bishop. *Levele* nodded in the direction of the black prisoner being led away to the pillory. "He's more than a political trouble-maker," said the Bishop. "I believe that you've captured *the Boogie Man!*"

The *Intendant* looked intrigued. "*The Boogie Man?*" he said.

Abel Freeman might as well have been the King of England as much as Bishop *Levele* was concerned. At last, he had the chance to teach his flock with a true scapegoat. "*The Boogie Man*," repeated the Bishop. "He creeps into houses after midnight and kills the men and boys while their asleep. He slits their throats. And then he rapes the women and girls. Sometimes he stabs them before the raping. He wounds them for several reasons."

"What reasons?" inquired the *Intendant*, his own perverted curiosity aroused.

"Wounded, his victims are more vulnerable, easier to manipulate, and less likely to escape," elucidated the Jesuit. "Also, the injured body is extremely sensitive to touch and the afflicted female is likely to cry and moan in pain, exposing a sense of her sensuality for his sadistic pleasures. He enslaves them."

Bigot pronounced sentencing: "He'll be hung from the gallows."

"Wait. That's not all," continued the Bishop. He situates the dead males around the room to watch his lust fest. They become receptacles for his Voo Doo Zombies, the living dead who feast on the blood and souls of his victims. The Zombie soul inhabits a corpse. It's Africa's religion transplanted by slaves to the *West Indies. The Boogie Man* is possessed by *the Devil!* He must be publicly exorcised before death or he might arise from Hell as, – King of the Zombies!"

"Will you drive *the Demon* from him before he dies,"

queried *Bigot,* feigning piousness. *Cadet,* engrossed in *Levele's* explanation, listened with rapt attention.

"We must send for a specialist," said the Bishop holding up his index finger. "*Friar Dominique Du Louches,* a refugee monk from *Acadia.* The Black Man will confess his crimes and sins, and denounce his Voo Doo Zombies and their dark master, *The Prince of Evil. Du Louches* has served under *a Spanish Inquisitor* on *the Iberian Peninsula.* He'll make this self-proclaimed Zombie King beg to be put to death."

"*The Boogie Man's* death shall be a public spectacle. Let it instruct and warn all slaves and villains," pontificated the *Intendant.* "*Cadet*! You're responsible for both exorcism and death!"

Bigot continued: "Assist his Excellency, the Bishop *Levele* and his monk *Du Louches.*"

Earlier after *Montcalm* had gone out of the room, the guards had blindfolded Jack, again. But he could see his own feet beneath the cloth binding, as he was steered outside and shoved towards the prison. The guard's torch lit the way. Upon the cobbled walkway next to a wall lay a dead bird, (*a Black-capped chickadee*). Within ten-inches of the fallen feathered-creature, a purplish wildflower on a thin, almost translucent stem had sprouted up. Jack interpreted the diminutive entities of *Fauna* and *Flora* as symbolic expressions of Reincarnation. A portent supported by memory and perception. All is in flux, for the *Wheel-Of-Life* is turning. A beautiful life exists ahead for him.

The hoodwinked British espionage prisoner, Royal Marine, Major Jack Wales stumbled forth, and the black handkerchief that shaded his eyes unloosed, and fell to the feet of the young woman coming round the corner. 'Dressed to kill', with tall, bouffant powdered wig, Mink Stole, and low-cut evening gown, she held her long-gloved hand at her bejeweled neck and over her heart (not unlike some artist's portrayal of Christ's Mother during the Annunciation), a star-struck, – Karen Bluejeans!

CHAPTER V.

'**M**agnificence personified', salaciously described the young woman exposing her cleavage, as she bowed before the captive Englishman to pick up his black scarf, which had been blinding him but now lay at her feet. Jack smiled his twinkling blue eyes. Karen Bluejeans could barely see any difference between them and the sparkling stars sprinkling star-lite o'erhead, William Shakespeare's "blessed candles of the night." And as though in candlelight, he said, using his best French pronunciation: "*Merci, Mademoi*selle. *Vous etes tres gentile*." ['Thank you, Miss. You are very kind'.]

"None of that," commanded the Sargent, swatting the side of Jack's head; then, grabbing the kerchief, he added: "Stand back, lady. He's a dangerous pirate – a spy for England!"

Wales was run into the dungeon beneath the barracks of the *Chateau Frontenac*. His over-coat and uniform jacket were taken. A century-old prison-chamber confined him. Two more cells filled the cellar; Robert Stobo occupied one of the cages; the other remained empty.

Stobo spoke: "You're in trouble. They let me out sometimes because I'm a gentleman and an exchange prisoner. But I've heard the guards talking. The guillotine is too good for you, too quick. They count on hanging you for piracy and spying."

"As long as they do it after I've gotten a little sleep," Jack wryly replied. A canvas cot upon a wooden frame offered him repose. He was too tired to make small talk or even to think about escape. But before losing consciousness, he thought of Billy and Abel. And he wondered: 'who was the un-chaperoned, good-looking gal all dressed up, out on the street, tonight?'

Karen Bluejeans had been without an escort, namely *Jacques-Pierre*, because he had deserted her at the last minute. Weapons had been issued to the *Musketeers* late that afternoon; and he had inspected each one personally. On the night of *the Governor's Ball*, the sixteen-years-old leader handed out guns to the older members of the Latin Club militia assembled in the Seminary's Central Hall. Younger boys were there to practice drill with wooden sticks. Timothy, a Second Grader, acting out how he would inflict hurt by breaking the Back of the British hit a broom in slow motion against an upright chair, to his maxim:

"Spare not a strong rod to bruise down the Redcoat!"

The Blue Musketeers of the Blessed Virgin roared a cheer of triumph. Thus their *elan* or *esprit de corps* had begun to form. Since they had not yet any elements of ammunition, *Jacques-Pierre* held his musket like a quarterstaff to demonstrate how to attack enemy infantry: "Regardless of rank!" All the others practiced their skill, except Fifth Grade John, whose knuckles got smashed." Holding hands in a circle *the Musketeers* screamed: "One for All! All for One!"

'Soon we will prove ready,' they believed, 'for combat against our adversary, the Anglo-Saxon Protestants'. Impassioned with the reception of guns, *Jacques-Pierre* had neglected to notify Karen Bluejeans of his inability to attend the Ball. However, she was not unaccustomed to his general failure at social events. Instead, she asked questions to herself about the prisoner. Her father could learn the whole story tomorrow and bring her up to date, since Eskimo provided wood for the barracks as well as for most of the other government and military buildings.

Josef the Woodcutter heard the report and informed his daughter of what had happened. Next she had him arrange for her to receive permission to visit the prisoner that she might take food as an Act of Christian Charity. She arrived with a basket for the Jailor and a basket for the handsome pirate, Jack Wales.

Down the dank, steep steps she stepped, until she came to the basement opening, where she stopped to stand upon some broken nails, which she felt underfoot. Her presence in the doorway created suspense for the two prisoners. And then she made her entrance.

Half of a long sandwich and some coffee for Stobo, the picnic basket and all the rest of its contents went to the Englishman:

"Eat," she said. "My name is Karen Bluejeans. Are you really a pirate?"

"No," answered Jack, perusing through the lunch. "I'm an English warrior who became lost in the fog. I was wearing my Uniform Redcoat. Where are the men who were with me?"

"Oh," said the girl. "The black man is full of *the Devil*. Once *the Demon* is driven from him, they plan to burn the poor African at the stake. They're already takings bids for what individuals get the honor of placing a faggot upon the bonfire's death flames."

"Your speak English well," said Jack, from behind jail bars.

"I learn at the Ursuline Convent school. Our teacher lived in *Le Havre* on the English Channel. Your French is excellent."

"I know Paris," he replied.

"I must go," she said, emptying the basket's contents . "I'll come again tomorrow with soap, blankets and some good food. And hopefully I'll have news of your friend."

"William Jones is his name. We called him Billy Boy, because he is so charming."

"Hopefully, we'll have information about your *charming Billy*," she said.

As she walked away, Jack called out after her: "*Merci, encore une fois, Mademoiselle, Karen Bluejeans.* " [Thanks again, Miss Karen Bluejeans.]

Stobo said nothing, at first; then he stared intently at Jack, and said: "She's kind of young. Isn't she?"

Outside on the streets again, the juvenile mounted her pony and sauntered towards the *Saint Louis Gate* and Beaver Lodge. From an upper balcony of *the Chateau*, like a vulture lurked Bishop *Level*. Inside his truest heart and deepest soul, he died.

Since the 13th century, the Papacy had established overland Eurasian contacts with Mongolia. And by the 15th century, the Portuguese had sailed to China's southeastern coast. Co-founder of *the Society of Jes*us, St. Francis Xavier attempted to convert the Chinese, but he was not allowed onto the mainland of *the Celestial Empire*.

Levele arrived at the Jesuit China Mission in *Peking*, where he studied Oriental languages and doctrines of Buddhist, Taoist and Confucian teachings, in 1734. He wrote brilliantly and at great length in the Jesuit *Relations* about his studies and also about the incredible wonders of China's ancient civilization, which had withstood the erosion of thousands of years.

One fateful day he watched the arrival of nomadic-like horsemen entering *the Forbidden City*, the Emperor's residence near *the Imperial City* that housed *the Potentate's* retinue. Among the riders of the shaggy ponies rode a young female, whom he later discovered came as *envoy extraordinary* or minister plenipotentiary, *a Chinese Mongolian Princess*. Unbelievably infatuated with the girl, the Jesuit scholar immediately sought an audience with her. She shunned him. Her religious affiliation sympathized with *Tibet's Dalai Lama*. Later, municipal police found the missionary just outside *the Gautama Buddha Temple*. Frothing at the mouth and slapping around on the ground, like a fish out of water or an epileptic suffering a *grand mal* seizure, *Levele* experienced something unexplainable.

The physicians diagnosed him as having had a nervous collapse that had followed a vivid hallucination, in which, the statue of Buddha had started to laugh aloud at him; and then, the laughing Buddha began to multiply in both directions of the horizontal axis, finally diminishing into a *d infinitum.* Laughing eyes winked at him. They knew about his elusive sorceress, the slanted-eyed seductress and high-cheek-boned, Royal Mongol. Vatican recalled the young priest to *Paris* for re-education and for preparation to guide New France as its righteous moral leader. Already, Adultery, Divorce, licentious living and all behavior against the Ten Commandments was not condoned in Canada.

Now he had seen her again, or the materializing of her likeness in the Mic-Mak girl riding home upon her pony, *Paint.* Bishop *Levele* commanded Mother Superior *Marie Etienne* to send the young maiden for spiritual examination at his Confessional. He gloated: "I'll have her!"

A piercing sleet-like rain fell and inhibited Karen Bluejeans from visiting Jack in gaol; she stayed absent from school; and she absolutely refused a visit of confidentiality to *Levele*. She did however enlist *Golden Bear* to help find what had become of Billy Jones. Several days later, the Huron youth returned to talk with her. They conversed in low undertones, like lovers at tryst.

Before going home, he said: "Karen Bluejeans, at present, the white men are more numerous than in my childhood. Soon they'll equal the leaves on the trees and stars in the skies. Come with me now and be my true love. And we shall dwell away elsewhere without them."

But she could not kiss him on the lips. He stormed off. And she prepared a luncheon basket for Jack. While Wales ate, she explained: "Billy Boy was tenderized by women in an Indian village up the river. They put seashells that pinched him until he was an oozy slime of blood and pus. They scalped him. They braised him, alive. All the while they kept asking him to choose his mother from amongst them. Finally, he died. Then they ate his body."

"He was a like a kid brother to me," Jack said, no longer eating.

"Your black brother is chained in a pantry box beneath the kitchen at *the Castle*. It's kept a secret so *the Devil* can't do any mischief among good people," she told him.

"Karen Bluejeans, why do you help me?" he questioned.

"I like your beautiful blue eyes," she said, giggling.

Abel Freeman could not see anybody through his eyes, which had been burnt out by a white-hot poker, to assist in deceiving *the Devil*: "*Satan* cannot do as much wrong when he doesn't see what he's doing," taught the Exorcist. Also the risk of escape was greatly reduced. *Du Louches* himself slept on a wooden bench next to Abel's black hole. Such was the dedication, zeal and self-sacrifice of the fat Friar, who mainly from over-eating frequently burst out with flatulence. He ate and drank to offset pain due to his missing left hand that he had lost while teasing at a Bear-baiting event. A velvet glove encased a wooden-fist or an iron-fist substitute.

"Mxyrztl yesoplat!" Often he would stay up all night whispering nonsensical words in funny voices to the black man. He had been trying to trick Freeman into conversing with the pseudo-demons. And sometimes to please the Bishop *Levele*, *Du Louches* invented vicious invectives and dirty little anecdotes that he attributed to this prisoner. The *ex-Acadian* 'Religious' always enjoyed talking with a Negro accent when reporting Abel's doin's: "In four or five weeks our interrogation should have his intolerant arrogance exhausted from him," predicted, the sweaty Inquisitor. He farted hard.

"Mxyrztl!" *The Devil* did less wrong-doing when wearily confused in a trap.

Wolfe discovered upon his return to England that Orders had been sent for him to remain in North America, and he apologized for his presence in *Angleterre*. He was summoned by dinner invitation to meet with the Prime Minister William Pitt close to Christmas Eve, 1758. Outside the PM's front door, amidst softly falling snowflakes, the merrymaking sounds of a well-dressed Quartet singing Yuletide Carols filled the air:

"God rest ye merry gentlemen. Let nothing ye dismay.
Remember Christ our Savior was born on Christmas Day,
To save us all from Satan's power when we have gone astray.
O! Tidings of comfort & joy! – comfort & joy! . ."

Previously, William Pitt, as Secretary of State and Leader of the House of Commons, said: "I am sure that I can save this country, and that nobody else can." A War Hawk in control of foreign affairs, Pitt wanted destruction of New France's authority in America, defeat of the French Navy everywhere, and world-wide ruin of France's opportunities, principally in India and Africa. Above all he worked to make England – Lord of the Seas!

Unacquainted with strong Port, an inebriated Wolfe accepted Pitt's commission to command the British land forces on the St. Lawrence River. Final designation to capture Quebec City awaited the opening of sealed orders secretly sent from King George II. The Sovereign's initials signed the Doom. The General flourished his sword, *Unicorn*, and rapped the sabre upon the dining room table like a Cossack. After James had left, Mr. Pitt commented to Mr. Temple, the guest there: "I'm beginning to question my own sagacity in appointing that young man."

Before leaving the country, Wolfe allocated time to see his father and mother and Catherine. His father, Lieutenant-General Edward Wolfe had served with dignity but without particular distinction. His mother, Henrietta Thompson hovered over her firstborn son, especially since the death of the younger boy, Eddie. Nonetheless, she approved of James's sweetheart, the tall, alabaster-complexioned, brunette Catherine (or Katherine) Lowther. Although they had not formally engaged, they had exchanged gifts of personal devotion. And when he should return from the fight in America they planned to wed.

'Twas at an evening party given by a friend of the Duke of Cumberland, son of King George II, when they first encountered each other. She enjoyed his Irish charm and Parisian wit, and she admired his Continental sophistication or *savoir faire* and his masculine seriousness; he beheld her beautiful nature in awed reverence, as the New Year commenced.

1759 was a year of miraculous occurrences, *the Annus Mirabilis*. In Germany, an amateur astronomer was the first person to cite the observation of an outer space event that related to cosmic significance, *Halley's Comet!* The comet was coming close to earth, its body composed of nebulous gas orbiting the sun, its head being of cloudy brightness and its tail sometimes stretching over 100 million miles long. Terror accompanied this celestial phenomenon. In London rioting broke out. People thought that the end of the world had come. *Broadsides* added fuel to the fires of mass hysteria by exposing that the *Bayeux Tapestry* (the embroidered chronicle of William the Conqueror's triumph at Hasting in 1066) indicated a comet hurling through the sky above the Norman warships. And at Julius Caesar's tragic death comets and stars had fallen from the firmament.

For James Wolfe, his time had come, too. Did the Comet hold special meaning for him? Although he was not superstitious, he chose not to ignore the comparisons made between the past and the present with respect to the solar happening. He believed that his Destiny, if written in the stars, should actualize itself on earth during or around the Comet's passage. Wolfe's sole purpose-of-existence now was to capture Quebec City and to free America of French tyranny. Was the accomplishment of this *Raison d'Etre* foretold by the Comet's visit?"

King George II was already decided and on record saying that if Wolfe were mad, then he [the King] hopes Wolfe will bite the other generals and make them mad also. Nevertheless, Wolfe did not have personal choice of all of his generals for the New France expedition. Both Brigadiers James Murray and Robert Monckton had served well with him before. But George Townshend, a wealthy gentleman who would rudely caricature Wolfe's portrait throughout the upcoming campaign, was more of a rival to the lean and hungry commander.

By March, Wolfe endured seasickness aboard flagship

Neptune, sailing to Canada as part of the biggest invasion fleet ever to disembark from *the British Isles*: 162 ships, 21 Ship of the Line, five Frigates, fourteen Sloops, two Bomb Vessels, a Cutter and 119 Transports fully loaded with 9,000 troops and materials.

Among the pilots to venture into the treacherous St. Lawrence River was navigator James Cook who should win fame as Discoverer of Australia, New Zealand, scattered South Pacific Islands, Hawaii, and North America's potlatch tribes of the Northwest Coast; and also, he found the Antarctic Ocean of the *Penguin* inhabited, South Pole. Cook like everyone else in the mighty force wore a black armband to commemorate the passing away of Wolfe's father.

Some French river guides were enticed aboard the leading British ship, which flew false flags. The river's passages then became common knowledge for the fleet. Captain Killick proposed that London's *Thames* was more deceptive and more treacherous than New France's so-called, slippery thorough-fare; and he concluded: "An Englishman will sail where no Frenchman dare to go." He communicated through a spreaking trumpet, like old *Triton* blowing his wreathed horn. Little ripples and currents of variegated hues also directed scouts of the Royal Navy like signposts along the way. Not one ship was lost as the fleet, helmed by Vice-Admiral Sir Charles Saunders, appeared opposite Quebec City's Lower Town off the small island *Ile d' Orleans*.

A tall, *Great Blue Heron* stood erect, arose his wings and flew up and away, as Lieutenant Meech with American Rangers, and the first of the Royal Marines secured the beach head. In- specting the towering cliffs of Cape Diamond and the multi-steepled skyline of *the City* through a telescope lens, Wolfe reflected that this must be the strongest enemy position in the world, an immovable obstacle blocking the passageway to a victorious Britain's trampling over the dictatorship of France's Canada.

Karen Bluejeans completed a restless passage herself that night. She remembered what Jack had said: "Don't come to me simply because of something superficial, such as the color of my eyes, or how much you enjoy looking into their blue. Come for my *Cause*, which is just." The rain beat upon the windowpane of her bedroom at *White Owl's Nest*. A tapping on the glass proceeded the tiny, knocking paw of the Gypsy's green monkey. When she let the creature in a gust of rainy wind entered too. She was drenched. The monkey crawled under her bed and slept there in a drawer. She moved to wake the verdant little fellow, but he was gone. Karen Bluejeans, herself, woke up wet from perspiration and released body fluids. With a deep sense of physical gratification she decided to tell Jack that she loves him.

'What is the *Cause* that Jack found so Just?' She pondered. Jack argued that England's Atlantic Seaboard Colonies felt imperiled by New France's Indians that raided along the frontier; secondly, the English colonies felt inhibited by the chain of French forts linking through the Ohio country down to New Orleans. Coupled with the *Adirondack* and *Appalachian Mountain Ranges, the forts hemmed in the British settlers, the families (men, women and children) and stifled human growth westward.

France posed as *Father* to the Native Americans, in contrast to Britain's role as their *Brother*. The very nature of the two relationships expressed the more democratic and liberty-or-freedom-loving equality inherent in the philosophy of the English. That is Jack's *Cause*. He wants Brotherhood and Liberty for all of mankind. He sought that to be her *Cause* now too. The *Cause* of Jack & Karen Bluejeans? *Democracy and Freedom for all Humankind!*

Wolfe's base camp on *Ile d'Orleans* next established a flanking post at *Point Levi*, where British artillery, giant how-itzers lobbed huge shells into the Lower Town of Quebec City; and much confusion and building damage occurred at once. However the camp was not immune to Foreign Terrorism! That unfortunate truth had been hinted at during the ocean-going voyage from England, – horrific rumors of savages torturing and their practice of Scalping.

Scalping never earned a reputation from ancient history, nor a precise description in European reports of the New World's warfare. Scalping was unique to the North American Indian. It most often took place after a prisoner's skull had been broken in by the assault of a stone tomahawk; then the killer knifed an incision 'round the hair' of his victim, from upper forehead to back of neck. Holding a foot on the shoulder of the defeated one, whose face had bit the dust, the scalper, with both hands, pulled the hair (or scalp) off from the dead man's head, usually from front to back. A war whoop ended the performance on an up-note.

Frenchmen in the wilds learned scalping along with other savage skills. And Americans learned how to scalp back against ruthless French raiders and their red-tribesmen. Bartering a scalp could sometimes redeem the dead. And though numbers of scalped individuals or whole communities grew in ten of tens, scalping did not always cause death. Around more than one hearth's burning log, a bald-pated story-teller thrilled a listener with a true confession of the breath-taking, near-Death escape from an Indian's bleeding knife-blade.

Massachusetts and other colonies offered a cash bounty for scalps of raiding Indians; and every frontiersman carried a

Scalping Knife sheathed in his belt or strapped to his boot or leather legging. Odds favored any sort of scalp, man's, woman's or child's, although scalps of male warriors won preference. On a fifty-fifty basis, a scalp torn in two pieces might earn a double claim for monetary reward. Large prize money for the scalp of a certain leader occasionally turned up. A collection of scalps exhibited the power and the wealth of the owner.

Mark Cronath, self-chosen Indian fighter once hung six or seven scalps from his burden belt; but he sold them because he believed that not only did they fail to provide innate strength for their carrier, but also instinct urged him to respect his person less through the hairs of dead men. He wasn't acting superstitiously. The scalps stood out, too much. They made him stand out, too much, also. Cronath liked a drab, inconspicuous, camouflaged look that blended into either a natural environment or a gentile tea parlor, without showing off any special ornaments or targets for the enemy. Cronath's attitude influenced Robert Rogers & his Rangers who sneak-attacked the French Indian village of *St. Francis* and killed hundreds of braves and their families in October, 1759. [Rogers wrote a code whose theme the American Green Beret later reflected].

French guerillas or their Indian allies (Algonkin, Huron, Ottawa, or other) slaughtered and scalped a British sentry. Night duty seemed a perilous period of deep, darkness or chaos. Wolfe increased watch-guard awareness, but still, the sentinels were jumpy. Oral history had sustained a fearful memory.

Fort William Henry (1757) surrendered to favorable terms after *Montcalm's* siege. British troops were granted arms and all honors, including Colours, to march away with the promise not to fight again on the North American continent. Sick and wounded were to be cared for by the French victor. But

Marquis de Montcalm, forty-four-years-old *Field Marshall* of France's military forces in Canada, failed to enforce safe passage and to control his savage allies. The Indians who felt betrayed by siege warfare, desired gifts for having gone on the warpath. They attacked the retreating troops, and the sick and wounded left in the fort's hospital. And they scalped and corpse robbed. *Montcalm* was aghast. Fort William Henry became synonymous with unearthly terror.

Wolfe's strengthened the morale of his sentries by instructing them to scalp back. He emphasized that his Order applied to only Indians and Canadians dressed as Indians. Cronath had suggested augmenting the directions by abducting children from a nearby village as subjects to practice on, for the Art and Science of Scalping. The renewed sense of unity among Wolfe's men fortified their courage, but the army trembled in anticipation of the uncivilized brutality of New France's Aborigine. Britain's soldiers had nothing to be ashamed of.

They were the best British Army of their time. Wolfe himself had trained them, and they practiced the Platoon Firing Technique regularly. Their primary weapon was the well tested musket affectionately referred to as *Brown Bess,* named after *Elizabeth I of England* and the *brawn's* gun walnut s*tock.* Most armies did not win battles by shooting; they bayonet charged. Frederick of Prussia devised flanking maneuvers that moved thousands of men upon the battlefield; but he too mostly won with cold steel. Wolfe's Redcoats firing *the Brown Bess* should hit targets up to seventy-five yards away. *Montcalm* had nothing to compare with them.

The French surpassed the British in total manpower, but Wolfe's fighting units (about 4,500) probably maintained a slight advantage of field numbers when matched against *Montcalm's.* Nevertheless, Wolfe needed to draw the French armed forces into the open outside the walls of Quebec City. Only then should his own platoons show their superiority.

Otherwise, only slow siege strategy should prevail. Like ancient catapults throwing boulders and plague-diseased corpses into the besieged castle courtyard, Wolfe's howitzers flung bombs at Quebec City's Lower Town, where a little less than one-third of the population lived.

Yet, starvation into submission, mining under the exterior fortifications, and propaganda for surrender were impractical to reasonable consideration. And a clean breach of a Quebec City wall for storm troops to rush through was next to impossible. However, since Canada was experiencing the second year of the worst harvest in the country's history, and dearth on a biblical scale was immanent, does not a classical siege have a relatively possible chance to win?

Troy fell to the Greek trickery of the *Trojan Horse*; and Jericho's walls collapsed apparently to the tune of the Hebrew God *Yahweh's* whim. Wolfe contemplated both of those lessons. Had not the 17th century, French military engineer, *Marshal Vaugban* theorized that the only sure way to survive being besieged demanded that the fortress must send out its soldiery to fight the attackers, once and for all? The most important factor though to consider was that the British Navy must leave Quebec City's *Bason* and the *River St. Lawrence* before Winter froze the waters and trapped the ships like beached whales or landlocked walruses; the fleet should not get caught as an armor-plated rhinoceros stuck in slow sinking quicksand. Quebec City must needs capitulation by end of September at the latest.

The French-Canadians feared the Royal Navy's devastating guns that had sunk the French Navy, coerced extermination of the fur trade and interrupted the flow of vital supplies from a France that had had 300 ships captured, in 1755. Such successful gunning contributed to England declaring war, in 1756. Wolfe kept Admiral Saunders' cannons as a kind of secret weapon, a reserve enforcement that did not consume ammunition by battering *the City*; but instead, the ordinance exercised deployment throughout the Siege Campaign, when covering troop movements, establishing beach-heads, and duplicitously screening major operations.

Naval guns measured up to 32 lbs. Army artillery, at best, fired a cannon ball of 12 lbs. Wolfe shot rocket-ship-shaped shells from 13-inches-wide Howitzers mounted at *Pointe de Levi,* directly across from the Lower Town. Local merchants cowered. And because no defensive parry existed to the Invasion Force's naval guns, Quebec City, to fight back, devised an aged, antique tactic, fashioned anew: – the Fire Ship!

Mediterranean navies of the ancient world, engaged in sea-war battles, had flung fire at enemy ships, and sometimes an oars-powered *Galley*, raging in flames, rammed the opponent fleet's flagship to wreck damage and to ignite panic; or *a scorch Bark* (a Fire Ship called a *'Hellburner!'*) acted as a non-discerning destroyer, undermining pyromaniac, and a 'Devil-May-Care' causer of confusion, self- detonated, showering incinerating explosives amongst the foreign foe's flotilla. Whether Anthony-and-Cleopatra's defeat at *Actium* (31 BC), or the *Spanish Armada's* debacle (1588), properly prepared Fire-Ships (with added combustible items and extra air-draft holes) when well inflated (with high winds, fast tidal current, and strong ebb flow) effectively aided naval victory.

Once Admiral Saunders began to unload big 32 pounders at *Pointe de Levi*, the Quebec City Council got up some Fire Ships to drive the English fleet away. They cost *Governor Vaudreuil* from 1-3 million *Marianne*; and the whole idea wasn't

to his liking. *Montcalm* spoke against the non-professional attempt to thwart the enemy, and the *Marquis* refused to partic-
ipate in the Fire Ships assault against the many British Men-of-
War anchored in the North and South Channels off the *Ile d'*
Orleans.

Therefore, command of the suicide vessels fell to those
men experienced in the ways of watercraft, fire-making and
the practicing of deceit. *Bigot's Cadet* made an illegal fortune
on the side, while community thought theorized that like the
sacred squalls sent through the Divine Intervention of *Our*
Lady of Victoires to sink the English Admiral Hovenden Walker
in 1711, "Right Makes Might!" Again, the City will be saved,
only this time by heavenly inspired Fire Ships' attacks.

Floating old ships and rafts loaded with powder and
scrap metal to go off hurtling wreckage and explosives into
England's navy comprised the Master Tactic. Such techniques
were still possible in 1759; but the French endeavor was not
properly directed. The ships exploded too soon, nine to eleven
miles before the targets. The sky flared with golden-red flames
and thick, black smoke. Explosives and projectiles flew all over,
but haphazardly packed they lacked destructive direction and
caused no damage; *Vaudreuil* had spent enormous wealth to
no avail.

Also, the Man-O'-War *the Sutherland* and its fellow warships, *the Centurion* and *the Porcupine,* blockaded traffic in
the Basin. And the British shore patrol and crew patrols rowed
their boats to tow away, with grappling hooks, the fire ships.
There was danger but no damage to British ships or service-
men. Three Frenchmen drown in their madcap, last minute
jumping off from blazing wrecks; others sustained burns and
injuries.

Saunders ordered Fireworks to be flared up, as a sign

of British superiority in foreign waters. Aboard flagship *Sutherland*, the Admirals and elite officers drank a toast for:

"British victory and a British flag over every port."

Wolfe experienced an epiphany over the amazing benefits attributable to a drink or good time among comrades. A final toast was taken to: "the King!"

After the Fire Ships had failed, Quebec City wearied with desperation. More than half of the Lower Town smoldered in ruins from the daily bombardment, which now also initiated a chipping away at the Upper Town. The City Council called upon the *Volunteer Home Guard*, almost 2,000 warriors strong, including the Seminary's Latin Club Militia, *the Blue Musketeers of the Blessed Virgin. Jacques-Pierre* was thrilled. This was his chance to make a name for himself, a name that should be repeated in the Throne Room of *Versailles*, the salons of Paris and the log cabins of Canada: "Jacques-*Pierre* of Quebec City because of his merit by arms is the man to serve as Governor of New France."

But to command the assault a hero was enlisted, *Jean-Daniel Dumas*. Rallying the French allied Indians, he had defeated Braddock back on July 6, 1755. Coldstreamer, Major-General Edward 'Lionhearted' Braddock, with his Virginia adjutant George Washington, was marching his expeditionary army of some 1,370 men (not including those with the oxen-drawn baggage-wagons and cattle) to take Fort Duquesne from the French. The fort had been built at the confluence of the *Ohio, Allegheny*, and *Monogahela* rivers. Equipped to hold about 200 troops, the fort was the key to controlling the Ohio country and trade down to New Orleans; but around 800 French armed forces (including more than 600 Indians) were stationed there, commanded by *Captain Claude-Pierre Pecaudy de Contrecoeur.*

Contrecoeur's troops had panicked upon hearing of the oncoming British force being led by pioneers wielding axes to make a road through the wilderness. However, he ordered *Captain Lienard de Beaujeu* to meet the enemy and curtail advancement of British goals. Encountering Braddock's advance guard, a little over 500 men under Colonel Thomas Gage, *Beaujeu* died in the first volley from the Redcoats. Second in command, *Dumas* pushed the defensive attack of 200 French Colonial Regulars (*Troupes de la Marine*) and Canadian Militiamen; more importantly, painted in green and *Monogahela*, mud-bottom brown, *Dumas* motivated the 600 some Indians *(Mingos, Delawares,Shawnees, Ottawas, Mississaugas, Wyandots and Potawatmis)* to attack.

Unlike a European army that wars upon an open battlefield, *the Fort Duquesne* fighters fought from behind trees, rocks and bushes; they fired from the flanks and shadows. The British though superior in numbers proved unprepared for woodland combat. They fell like swatted flies. And for the defenders winning became as easy as shooting fish in a barrel. Gage's advance guard retreated in a disorderly manner into the main body of British troops. Both Braddock and Washington had several horses shot out from under them. In the heat of the confusion and slaughter, Braddock was mortally wounded and bled out on the return journey. Washington buried him in the middle of the road, where retreating troops covered the grave to prevent desacralizing the corpse.

Only 459 of Braddock's army were not killed or wounded. All of the animals, wagons and big guns were lost. There was a moment when the Virginians could have taken high ground and altered the course of battle; but they were the sole group of English-speaking soldiers who had had experience fighting in Indian fashion; and they were unable to seize control of the events. The Indians killed, scalped and corpse robbed while screeching bloody murder. *Dumas* let them run wild.

The glory of victory associated with *Dumas* shone untarnished by the horrors of Indian savagery. They walked hand in hand together as mutual recommendations for his leadership in war. He planned to land with the Home Guard and then to go through the woods for a surprise attack against the British artillerymen.

Jacques-Pierre planned to spearhead the punitive pillage of the British camp at *Point de Levy*. Quebec City's Mayor would lead the main attack. The raiding force was from 1,500 to 1,800 warriors strong; the exact count was difficult to make because the composition of the volunteer army kept shifting; and even at the last minute before boarding the long boats, a sure number was not possible, because nightfall had arrived and it was too dark to tell how many of the Home Guard were present.

The tide was against the make-shift fleet of transports launched at midnight (July 15, 1759). Some vessels were not more than rowboats or simple canoes. And the winds blew askew, causing further navigational obstacles. Night obscured vision. It was black, as black as a black panther; it was as black as the bottom of a cannon barrel. Halfway across *the Basin* of Quebec, the Mayor turned around and returned to the Lower Town. About two-thirds of the boats did likewise, or they lost themselves up and down the St. Lawrence River. Yet close to 750 intrepid souls hit the north shore of *Point de Levy*.

An organized map of operations had not been drawn up, and nobody had any certain place to land. Lanterns and torches were forbidden, and in the darkness you couldn't see your hand in front of you. The beach was higher up than previously imagined, six or seven feet straight up like a rocky wall. And in the transferring from boat to shore several men drowned. More men cut, bruised and bloodied themselves on the rocks. A *Musketeer* met such a fate, only worse.

A kid of about six years old fell in the dark and the other boys stepped on him as they hurriedly struggled up the beach. None of them let him up. They trampled him to death. Who could tell where they were stepping? 'A real soldier steps on anyone who gets in his way', believed the eager-for-combat *Musketeeers:* "One for All!"

They had separated from *Dumas* and his bodyguard, but *Jacques-Pierre* knew that they should move into the woods; *Dumas* had spoken of a stone church or chapel for a rendezvous point at the forest edge. Unfortunately, the Latin Club Leader was unable to locate the tree line of the woods, and gunshots were going off everywhere in the darkness. He divided the group into two lines, and at his command each fired a volley. A boy cried out in pain: "I've been hit"

The British sentry had not yet sounded an alarm; therefore, the boy was injured by one of his own townsmen. Wild shooting kept popping off. *Jacques-Pierre* ordered a strategic retreat back to the boat. For encouragement, he shouted the slogan: "Better to fly and live to fight another day as a hero than take a stand and die like a nobody." That philosophy probably echoed better in Latin than Canadian-French; but it wouldn't make any difference. *Jacques-Pierre* like the others in his company may have gotten to the river, where no boats remained, but nobody knows. Not a scintilla was discovered of the Seminary's Latin Club Militia:

The Blue Musketeers of the Blessed Virgin.

Single shots and shouts continued to disturb the silence of the hour.

Dumas and a few boatloads of men filtered through the woodland trees to the Church. As in many small communities, the best and most strongly constructed building was the Church. A big guy from *Marseilles* smashed open the doors. Men followed, pushing their way in. *Dumas* shoved his way to the front of the altar.

"Plan! Decide! What should we do?" yelled one man.

"It's dark as hell out there!" a volunteer said. "We can't see anything. Let's get the hell out of here before we get killed!"

Dumas shook his head and replied, as musket balls began to hit the Church's outer walls: "We were over-confidant. We should have had scouting reports of this terrain and the disposition of the enemy."

"You didn't have any of that against English Braddock," argued one fellow. A window shattered.

"You are wrong," corrected *Dumas*. "And I led savages who were akin to nature's surroundings. But this is not the place; nor is it the time to discuss such matters."

A back door was unlocked and the party, the surviving main body of the punitive raid, fled. The majority of the British learned of the attack the next day. The front line sentries had platoon fired onto the river.

The City Council glumly received the report of the fiasco. *Vaudreuil* too was displeased, perhaps less by the defeat of *the Volunteer Home Guard*, and more because the *Marquis de Montcalm* should now justify determinations with the attitude that as *Field Marshall* he had already been proven right and should therefore rule unchallenged by *the Governor's* interference. Solemn High Mass was said for the dead; no exceptions were made for the *Blue Musketeers of the Blessed Virgin:* "One for All! All for One!"

Nor did Karen Bluejeans do more than sigh an exasperated sigh of sorrow for *Jacques-Pierre*. She stopped thinking of him. She now thought only of Jack.

Soon after, in the darkened dungeon, Jack Wales thanked Karen Bluejeans for her food basket, from which arose the fragrance of apples. He also acknowledged her avowal of love. Through prison bars, he kissed both of her cheeks. And she protested:

"Don't kiss me, as if I were a child or as though you were awarding a medal. Kiss me on my mouth, like an adult!"

CHAPTER VI.

*L*ouis-Joseph de Montcalm-Gozon, Marquis de Montcalm *de Saint-Veran*, a veteran of foreign wars, accepted command of the King's troops in North America, 1756. By 1759, he was second only to the *Governor Vaudreuil* and in charge of all matters *militaire* in Canada. To frustrate Wolfe's superior platoon firing system, he constructed eight miles of trenches, abates, *chevaux-de-faux*, parapets and other defenses, such as blockhouses, redoubts and so on, to protect the left flank of Quebec City from *Beauport* unto the 300 foot *Montmorency River Falls*. In July, from desperation Wolfe said that regardless of the Royal Navy, if necessary he will stay until November to take *the City*; Montcalm's reply:

"If necessary, I'll wait for you until June."

That Summer of 1759, with Wolfe's army camped more than 500 women to wash clothes and perform other duties, such as cooking, nursing and food scavenging. The soldiers themselves freshened the camp's straw on a diurnal schedule to make the grounds sweet smelling. An entertainment night was awarded to troops and camp women, the rationale being to live a little more than the everyday experiences (like an athlete in training stretching muscles) in order that the upcoming contest should not be lost because of stifling inhibitions. Everybody awaited the show with sincere anticipation. One's best clothing should be worn; and the women sought to outdo the next female, either with the sewing of original garments or through the arrangement of whatever attractive vestments they could gather. Couples formed, to go 'on a date' together. Attendants would serve Spruce Birch Beer, Hard Cider, Grog and Rum. Wolfe's alcohol policy was regularly very restrictive. And he considered camp women to be burdens. Nevertheless, ShannonYardley from the Halifax loading-dock's Tavern, *St. George & The Dragon* was publicized to play Spanish guitar and sing.

Erin the Red-Haired of Eire presiding as Mistress of Ceremonies entered onto the large stage that had been hastily erected under the supervision of Wolfe's Chief Engineer Patrick Mackellar. The leading lady walked in between two costumed actors: *the British Lion* (wearing a Crown, carrying a mace-like Scepter and holding a grand Orb) and *Britain's Unicorn!* (as if on leave from *the National Coat-of-Arms*). The two folkloric-like characters accentuated the Emerald-Isle's Redhead's sequined, shamrock-green dress, which scintillated, as she welcomed with choreographed body-language and theatrical facial-expressions of astonished surprise; finally, the audience's huzzah, cheering and cat-calls quieted down. Then came on Shannon Yardley. The beautiful young blonde stood on the apron of the stage and to her own guitar accompaniment sang, *"The Minstrel Boy:"* –

> "The minstrel boy to the war has gone.
> In the ranks of Death, you'll find him.
> His father's sword he has girded on,
> And his wild harp slung behind him. . ."

Looking like a radiant bride, dressed in white, she got a standing ovation and approving shouts of, "*Bravo!*" and, "*Encore!*" Though she had searched carefully in the crowd of faces below her, she had not seen Billy 'Boy' Jones. Suddenly, appeared *Monsieur La Grenouille*, a hunch-backed actor garbed as a fat, grape-green Frog; a Jester's Cap and a wine-colored Cape illustrating France's *Fleur-De-Lis,* he wore, as he jumped onto the stage to abduct *Erin the Red-Haired of Eire.* The crowd went wild: "Boo! Boo!" – "Hiss!" – "Villian!"

Like some sort of Punch-&-Judy Puppet Show, *the Lion* and *the Unicorn* rushed central stage to club down the yellowish-green Frog and to rescue their hostess, Ireland's rouge-tressed damsel in distress. As fast as the kidnapping had started, it ended with a struggling, loudly protesting *Monsieur Grenouille* resisting arrest in chains while being dragged away off of the stage.

"Sure enough!" chimed, the Mistress of Ceremonies, to audience applause.

And then wearing Scottish Kilt and Bearskin Cap, onto the stage marched the *42 Foot, Royal Highland Regiment, The Black Watch – Pipe & Drums* playing: "*Thick Lies the Mist on Yonder Hill.*" Garmented in her Clan's red-and-black-and-white Tartan-emphasized outfit, a bonnie girl with black braids danced the 'Dance-With-Swords'.

A Sword Swallower, a Fire-Eater, and a couple Jugglers of balls-&-pins amused the concert goers before heavy tramping boots announced the arrival of the next act. Featuring the running, *White Horse of Hanover,* the Grenadier (Miter) Capped *Band of The Coldstream Guards's* and *The Coldstream Guards' Drum-&- Bugle Corp* entered. A High Soprano who had had some Opera lessons, her backup of four women from various Sunday School choirs, and several strings (Violins and an orchestra Harp) found their way onstage to make music with the Conductor and ensemble of musicians already there for: *"Rule Britannia!"*

> *"When Britain first, at Heaven's command,*
> *Arose from out the azure main;*
> *This was the charter of the land,*
> *And guardian angels sung this strain:*
> *'Rule, Britannia, rule the waves;*
> *Britons never will be slaves.'. ."*

Younger sailors and soldiers stood close to the stage independently or in small squeezed-together groups. Male and female couples followed sitting on temporary benches. Ships' crews and regimental constituents filled the remaining space in back; around a total of 5,500 people had co-operatively crowded into the amphitheatre-like area for the concert. It should have been a larger audience, especially because the show was free and no tickets were required; but skeleton crews deducted from the gathering. Surrounding security was three ranks deep. The French were dug in on the other side of *the Montmorency Falls*. Though several miles away they may have heard the terminating stanza of Britain's unofficial anthem by James Thomas that was made popular nineteen years earlier through a *London Gentleman's* magazine, in1740: –

> ". . Blessed isle! With matchless beauty crowned,
> And manly hearts to guard the fair.
> Rule Britannia, rule the waves;

> "Britons never will be slaves.
> Rule Britannia! Britannia rules the waves!
> Britons never will be slaves."

The audience participation during the *Repetend* thundered like the ocean's crashing waves. Boats, to transport a large number of guests back to *the Ile d' Orleans*, awaited at the landing.

Red-Haired Erin of Eire returned to the stage holding hands with her escort, an actor clothed like a big Lobster. They introduced for a farewell *chanson*, Shannon Yardley, whom supported by the military band, pipes, drums, and bugles, sang: "*Wild Mountain Thyme*": –

> "O! the summertime is a-comin',
> And the leaves are sweetly a-turnin,
> And the wild mountain thyme is a-growin',
> All across the purple heather.
> Will you go, Lassie, – o? . ."

Off the river's bank, on deck aboard the frigate *HMS Starfish*, the First Mate gripped the upper-deck railing and asked: "When will the fireworks start up?"

"There's the signal, now, Sir," replied, the Chief Petty Officer, indicating a waving torch, which flashed like a streak of liquid gold in the night on the black hillside. The Lower Deck got underway to commence shooting pyrotechnics.

The fireworks began, as Shannon's tearful song was finishing the *Chorus*:

> ". . And we'll all go together
> To pluck wild mountain thyme,
> A-bloomin' 'crost the purple heaven.
> Ah, will you go, Laddie, – go?"

The Black Watch Bagpipes droned on the refrain over and over and over again.

Then the *Finale* commenced, including giving on stage, the *Presentation of Colours* for every regiment in the Invasion Force: –

15th Foot/ the East Yorkshire Regiment/ the Prince of Wales's Own Regiment of Yorkshire;

22nd Foot/ the Cheshire Regiment;

28th Foot/ Gloucestershire Regiment/ Royal Gloucestshire, Berkshire and Wiltshire Regiment;

35th Foot/ the Royal Sussex Regiment/ the Princess of Wales's Own Royal Regiment;

40th Foot/ the South Lancashire Regiment; the Queen's Lancashire Regiment;

43rd Foot/ the Oxfordshire and Buckinghamshire Light Infantry/ the Royal Green Jackets;

45rd Foot/ Sherwood Foresters/ Worcestershire and Sherwood Foresters Regiment;

47th Foot/ the North Lancashire Regiment/ the Queen's Lancashire regiment;

48th Foot/ the Northamptonshire Regiment/ the Royal Anglian Regiment;

58th Foot/ the Northamptonshire Regiment/ the Royal Anglian Regiment;

60th Foot/ the King's Royal Rifle Corp/ Royal Green Jackets;

Fraser's Highlanders.

And proudly standing with them were *Erin the Red-Haired of Eire, the Lion & the Unicorn*, the Lobster, Fire-Eater, Sword Swallower, Jugglers, Swords Dancer, Shannon Yardley and all the Musicians, who as fireworks flared, delivered, *the National Anthem*: –

"God save great George, our king,

Long live our noble king, . ."

At the commandeered farmhouse that served as General Headquarters, Wolfe consumed *Opium* to relieve his maladies. He deferred his incandescent, golden-hued visions of forgotten empires, their monumental architectural-edifices arising and crumbling back down into minutia, only to arrive again only higher than before, like rebuilding a child's sand castles washed away in the foam of a surf, somewhere on the nocturnal shore of eternity; and he writhed to ignore the other distractions of the opiate. He had heard most of the concert's music and in constant discomfort he agonized about the forthcoming attack on *Montcalm's* eight miles of defense-works.

Malaria, "bloody flux," or diarrhea from dysentery afflicted many British soldiers, and almost half of the invasion force personnel had some illness or injury. Wolfe standing by the window watched the last of the excited pink fireworks burst in the distant sky, as he listened to the cessation of the instruments and voices singing *the Anthem*. He heaved a deep breath, sighed and buried his face in his hands.

Karen Bluejeans prepared a culinary delight for Jack and herself. Food fare was limited to small portions that she might carry all of the seafood dinner in one large, overflowing picnic basket. Hot Clam Chowder served as *the Entrée,* following *Hors-d'Oeuvres* (a crunchy cracker smeared with cooked Cod and topped with a black olive). The main course was Cold Lobster with Coral Sauce, heated French Bread and Vegetable Salad (a combination of cooked lobster tails and claws, torn fresh lettuce, chunks of cucumber and a quarter of a dozen Pinto Beans).

The Pinto Beans were included to especially honor her Pinto pony, *Paint.* The Coral Vinaigrette contained the liquid from steamed Lobster, wine, water and a few drops of extra-virgin olive oil. Spinach and a little bowl of buttered, baked, baby-potatoes and a handful of blueberries and raisons went with the First Course. Two luscious Oysters with Truffle Sauce were offered as a Second Course to the captured mariner. Desert for the salty meal was sweet *Mousse au Chocolate* (chocolate pudding). A couple bottles of white wine, a small block of Swiss Cheese and some young goat cheeses, (*Roguefort and Camembert*), hard Maple Syrup candy and a tangerine completed the repast, save for Tawny Port, and a snifter of *Cognac* to sip along with a cup of coffee.

As always, she had set a second basket for the Guardroom, and a treat for *Circumflex* the prison cellar cat; and also, she had cloth-napkin-covered a bread-basket of seafood for Stobo. Perhaps that initiated her opening remark to Jack?

"Where's Robert?" she inquired.

"He never came home, last night," replied Jack. "Now and then he stays over, – if he is too drunk to travel, or something like that."

Carrying a satchel of Indian pemmican (dried lean meat mixed with fat) and a water canteen, Captain Robert Stobo, security hostage for George Washington, had escaped towards New York.

"Well you can keep his dinner for a snack later," she said slipping off her Baby Harp Seal Shrug, throwing back her head of lustrous, chestnut-black hair and flashing her mouthful of perfectly-sculptured teeth. Jack observed that she was wearing a sleeveless dress of turquoise tint, a string of moon-white pearls and a longer necklace of darker pearls like colored, wooden beads. Her face was framed within each of her pierced ears by a long dangling ear-ring of a Storm Petrel's feather attached with a wire like a fishing hook into Wampum bead clusters. On her right arm a shiny brass bangle with copper-edged borders held an incised whale emblem. She wore several golden bracelets on her left wrist and three, salmon-pink pearl ankle-bracelets. Soft leather sandals shod her feet, which were adorned with sea-green toenail polish and a silver toe-ring. Incarnadine-colored lipstick glowed, when she said:

"The theme of tonight's dinner is *La Mer*," [The Sea]. She passed, with *Hors-d Oeuvres,* a cork-screw and a bottle of white wine for Jack to open. "I couldn't procure *Champagne,*" she admitted. "There wasn't any at *White Owl's Nest* and Pena has chained-&-locked the wine-cellar cage at *Chanticleer*." She put her fingertips over her mouth in realization of the *faux pas* she may have made mentioning the locked and chained cage. But he only noticed her sea-green fingernail polish. She provided the cat with a bowl of tiny bathing tadpoles. Curiosity aroused the fluffy feline creature who mewed, "*Merci*."

Jack sat cross-legged on a Hudson Bay Company white wool, Indian trade blanket of three stripes (red, yellow, and brown), which was worth twenty beaver pelts. He politely began to feast, unlike the two guards whose chowing-down had caked their faces with pinkish-yellow Lobster stuffings.

Karen Bluejeans spread a white cotton, double-ply quilt, which with, Embroidery & Applique displayed in silk, satin and velvet, – three concentric circles: swimming red fish, swimming green turtles and swimming purple fish; those ocean denizens framed a *Tondo* illustrating a realistic, rufous-hued *Curlew Sandpiper* standing in a very, very shallow pool of French blue; a sea-green tinted, sea-shell-patterned ribbon trimmed her blanket's borders: conch (chalkish yellow) – marlinspike (Prussian pink) – scallop (creamy beige) – bivalve (pastel green), and – triton (baby blue). The water-color-like illumination of the sea-shells reflected the multihued, *Shore*

Bird positioned in the *Centre*. Though child-like, the perceivable visual effect of the quilt's brilliancy was similar to that of the translucent radiance refracted within a stained-glass window, like the gorgeousness of *Chartres Cathedral's* rose windows in France.

She sat down to serve their dinner by candlelight, (which incorporated using her family's best French China and silver) with the captive Englishman. Neither knew that Captain Robert Stobo had escaped. He had simply accompanied his host out of *the City* and onto the trails towards New Hampshire and later New York, where he should report that Jack Wales, though alive, was languishing in prison. Karen Bluejeans ladled soup into Jack's soup bowl.

Jack enjoyed her companionship as they ate, and many pleasantries were interchanged during *le diner*. Over selection of cheeses, the Indian maiden suddenly said: "Oh, I forgot to tell you, something important."

"Pray tell, lovely maiden," proposed Jack.

"Abel Freeman is going on trial for playing the Devil's fool. Trial by Ordeal! Will the judgment fire consume him?" she asked.

"Or will an angel of the Lord intervene with the substitute of a ram?" continued Jack. "Abel was a good man. That black rookie reminded me of Roland, my servant who joined Wolfe's service with the Duke of Cumberland in Germany. The orderly was pulverized by shot enemy cannon-shell while holding the bridle of James's horse in battle." Jack looked forlorn.

"Mousse au Chocolate! for dessert," interjected, Karen Bluejeans, changing the mood.

Their dinner conversation turned to England and Jack's memory of his youth in Cornwall at the tip or toe of the island, where white, seahorse-shaped wave-crests rode into the foamy, salt-water-streamed strand of damp beach grains. It was Karen Bluejeans, who charmed by Jack's description of his boyhood, changed the subject to the bedroom stories of her own child-hood. Putting a stray Pinto Bean into Jack's salad bowl, she said: "There. Now I'll remember where I've been, so I won't get lost in the woods."

Jack snorted a laugh, and said: "Nursery-room fables rarely exceed that concept. An unique Cornish tale however is called: *Jack and the Beanstalk!* Have you heard it, O! Planter of the Pinto Bean?"

"Uh-uh," she said, nodding her head to signal negation. "Is it about you, my lord?"

"It's about a poor boy who trades the family cow for al-legedly magic beans," he began. "The beans planted like seeds grow up into a beanstalk that climbs into the clouds. Jack scales up the enormous stem, slays the giant ogre, takes the stolen treasure and the singing harp of gold, and slides home, where with axe he cuts down the Beanstalk. Everybody in the kingdom lives happily ever after."

"Good! Good! Very Good!" exclaimed Karen Bluejeans, sitting up and clapping her hands. She had been lying on her side with one hip high along the horizon of her body's figure. "You told it like it was your story." Dessert was almost over.

"I wish it were," said he. "Quebec City is like a giant's treasure trove in the sky; but there isn't a Beanstalk for Jack to get away upon."

They laughed. Then after a kiss through the bars, Karen Bluejeans, said:

"Maybe you do have a Beanstalk?"

Jack while picking up miscellaneous dinner items, said: "Go on. I'm listening,"

"A path exists that is like a big tree rooting on the riverbank and branching into Quebec City. It's very narrow like a secret passage; but it's really just an old goat trail that only a few washer-women still trod up and down."

"Where is the location of your secret passage?" asked Jack.

"It's about five kilometers [two or three miles] from here. It begins in a little cove down by the river and it comes out at the top onto the Plain of Abraham," the girl said, providing the information like a scout. She licked the last of chocolate pudding from her desert spoon.

"Five kilometers!" Jack Wales could not believe his ears. "Could an army travel this pathway?" he questioned.

"Sure," said Karen Bluejeans.

"Karen Bluejeans, stand up, listen carefully. Answer me truly," Jack said, slowly and solemnly. "Is the passage wide enough for General Wolfe to lead the Invasion Army onto the Plains of Abraham. There he will have high ground to shoot down into Quebec City. 'Yes,' means British victory."

"Yes!" she said. And in so saying, she realized that she was betraying *the City*. All of the people and things – her father Josef the Woodcutter, Pena, Ortiz, her priest Father Greyrobe, her Godparents Joan and *Jacques-Louis*, *Bonhomme* Simon, Sister *Marie Etienne*, the good nuns at the Ursuline Convent School, and *Bernadette, Michelle, Patricia, Jacqueline, Colette*, the Twins and her other classmates, *Madelaine de Repentigny, Intendant Bigot*, Joe *Cadet, Governor Vaudreuil*, Bishop *Levele*, the *Chevalier Marquis de Montcalm and* the French Army and the Canadian Army, even *Versailles's Madame Pompadour* and *King Louis XV* & France, and Canada and all the citizenry and everybody else, and everything else – her father's altar piece in *Holy Child Chapel*, and his statue of the Virgin, her doll *Brigit, White Owl's Nest*, and Beaver Lodge and all of the Upper Town and the Lower Town, their shops and homes and buildings were being sacrificed for the personal approval of Jack Wales; she had answered him truly with their shared belief in the English Atlantic Seaboard Colonies' democracy and brotherhood of liberty and equality, – *Democracy and freedom for all humankind!* Like a bride affirming her wedding vow, she again said: "Yes!"

Jack took her arm and pulled her close to the bars. They kissed each other again. Her head turned. She said: "I forgot to tell you something else. The British held a party at *Montmorency Falls,* last night. Music and fireworks galore. My father says that soon they will attack to take *Beaufort* and *the St. Charles River.*"

In the blink of an eye, Jack comprehended that he must escape to notify Wolfe of the precious secret passage!

"*Montcalm's* deeply entrenched there," replied Jack. "Much blood shall spill. I must escape. You must risk all if necessary to help me escape, as soon as possible."

"Let me go, to speak with my father, and the people at Beaver Lodge," she whispered. "We'll plan a way out for you. Maybe my father can get you a parole like Captain Stobo's?"

The lovers said good-night. Karen Bluejeans then departed through the smokey guardroom into the night air. Ortiz was patiently waiting for her in the cart drawn by the old mules *Alec* and *Heloise.* The girl put the baskets and blankets into the cart-bed and climbed on board before he could assist her.

"Tiz,' she said, "if you wanted to leave *the City,* how would you do it?"

"I am going to leave," he said. The cart-wheels turned on the pavement. "I'll go past *Montreal* and down south by river to New Orleans. And from there I'll sail away back home to Mexico. Quebec City's kingdom is crumbling."

The next morning Karen Bluejeans helped the housekeeper

make Josef breakfast at *White Owl's Nest*. She asked him if he would help Jack.

"I can't help, sweetie-girl," said Josef in between fork-fuls of scrambled eggs, toast, Canadian Bacon and hot potato slices. "I've already inquired on behalf of your Jacob. And the answer is:

'No!'" He took a sip of black coffee. The breakfast smells wafted the air.

"No. He cannot have a pardon, because his crimes are piracy and espionage. They're too serious to excuse. The death penalty is in abeyance only for *Montcalm's* desire to exploit a prisoner exchange. As for a parole? Ha! Even I laugh." He wiped his mouth with the red-&-yellow checkered napkin, pushed his breakfast plate away, and hugged his coffee mug in his hands like a poor man in a soup kitchen.

"*Vaudreuil* won't issue a parole status because Jack has been deemed untrustworthy. Did you know that he tried to escape when first captured?"

"Oh, Eskimo!" said Karen Bluejeans calling his old cog-nomen, which she hadn't used in years. "Every prisoner-of-war is required to try escaping. If you get Jackie a parole, he will probably be okay, – thankful to be out of the hole." She wore a white A-line dress with ruffles and a silk yellow ribbon.

"I can't help," replied Josef.

"Well, I'm going to help him," she said, tightening a fist in her hand.

"Good Luck!" said her father, as he rose from the table. "Don't do anything rash."

The tall, young girl walked towards Beaver Lodge. She noticed the many people on the streets and the unusual con-gestion at *the St. Louis Gate*. 'Oh, yes,' she said, to herself, 'the trial by ordeal begins today.' The trial was really just a part of the pseudo-exorcism of Abel Freeman. *De Louches* was pretty sure that he had driven *the Devil* out of the black man; but he couldn't be absolutely positive. Will *Voo* Doo prevail? 'Trial by Ordeal' should finalize all doubts, as well as soothe the starving population. Even though New York shippers smuggled goods to Canada for Yankee profits, their French-Canadian enemy was enduring great deprivation.

Ship's Bells rang 10 A.M., when Major-General James Wolfe assembled Brigadier Generals, (Robert Monckton, James Murray, and George Townshend) in the Captain's Cabin aboard Vice-Admiral Sir Charles Saunders's brevet flagship, *The Prince of Wales.* At anchor in the South Channel of the *Ile d' Orleans,* the ship rode the deep, navy-blue brine, which streaked pale aquamarine, black, pink, yellow-green and white rivulets like splashy stripes of sunshine-treated, water transmutations. A yellow-billed, orange-legged seagull flying past the Man-of-War's stern seemed to be smiling while shrilling his call of low, flat monotone notes: "Klooh, Kloaw, Kaaw!"

A long pennant, painted with St. George's Red Cross, clung to the pinnacle of the weathered Ship-of-the-Line's mainmast. A minor breeze barely quivering in the rigging blew stronger through an open window below deck. And a draft was felt by the temporary inhabitants of the crowded cabin. Aside from Wolfe and the Brigadiers, also present were Sir Charles, himself, several Naval Officers and the Invasion Force's Chief Engineer Patrick Mackeller.

Major-General Wolfe cleared his throat, and began: "Gentlemen thank you for your presence here this afternoon. And thank you for the reply of your written opinions concerning my plans for an amphibious assault upon *Montmorency*. We've all had some time to re-think the pre-determinations. And now, I request your verbal conclusions."

"The operation reeks of reckless endangerment. Our troops won't be coming out of it alive," spoke up James's friend, General Monckton.

"It's a gamble with the odds greatly against us," said, General Murray.

"Absurd!" replied, General George Townshend, haughtily.

"The British Navy cannot direct the trajectory of its guns high enough to knock out any of the possible French defenses along the upper ridges of the shore," said, Vice-Admiral, Sir Charles Saunders in a voice of reasonable caution. "And *Montcalm* is well situated."

Finally, Mackeller gave his observations. "I agree with the Admiral said the Chief Engineer. "*Montcalm* won't come out and fight you on level ground. He is going to hide in his holes like a badger. And you'll not flush him out. This isn't *Louisburg*. There isn't any ground for us to place our artillery. We must start up river and go from *Cap Rouge* in the opposite direction, – West to East, instead of invading from the East at *Montmorency* to Quebec City in the West."

"Thank you," Wolfe said. "Are there any additional comments?" Further commentary was quit.

"We will attack, then," continued, General Wolfe. "We can't cross the river and attack from *Cap Rouge* because the French Army of Canada would march from *Montreal* and assault our rear guard and main force, while we're moving the twenty miles to *Montcalm's* forces at *the City*. We should have to fight on two fronts, and they would undoubtedly crush us." Silence reigned except for the crying of river birds outside the flagship's Captain's Cabin. "Nor do we have a more conservative card to play than to attack Quebec City on this side of *the Falls* and *River*," went on Wolfe. Once we've established a beach-head we can capture *Beauport*, cross the *St. Charles* and maneuver around behind *the City* to fire down into the Upper Town." Wolfe looked visibly distressed, but added:

"Armed-to-the-teeth, our antagonist cunningly dug himself in behind ditch, palisade and battery fortifications, so that I cannot get at him without spilling a torrent of blood, and that perhaps to no purpose. *The Marquis de Montcalm* is at the head of a great number of bad soldiers [14,000], and I am at the head of a small number of good ones [5,000]. But we cannot delay longer. The Royal Navy can't linger. The soldiers have had a week to sharpen themselves since the music-&-fireworks concert. They are impatient enough to storm hell."

Muttering regrets the high command acquiesced to the plan for an attack tomorrow morning. The meeting was adjourned and the participants attended to their responsibilities. Gently in between the banks of the riverine channel rocked *The Prince of Wales.*

'We cannot wait until morning's light,' thought Karen Bluejeans. 'Jack and I need to escape at nighttime, when we can hide under a cloak of night-dark stars. First though, I must consult Pena'. She began to browse around the yards and the barn at *Chanticleer.* Beaver Lodge had refused to donate or to sell firewood for the 'Trial by Ordeal'.

'Trial by Ordeal' was an early system of justice among human creatures. If the victim survived the trial/ ordeal then he was innocent. Judge and jury employed a variety of different techniques: fire; water; poison; emaciation; confinement, exile and others. Fire was the most popular since it offered flashy movement and exciting sounds; and the suffering was immediately evident with burns and painful exclamations. Scalding water, boiling oil and all forms of cooking counted under the Fire category. Stab wounds or tool-inflicted injuries, drowning and freezing, kept separate conditions, as did poisoning, star-vation, *et cetera*.

Exorcism sometimes required all the different styles of 'Trial by Ordeal' to chase away *Satan*.

Plus, the victim might need examining to make sure that he had been purged of *the Evil One*. It all added up. But most often, the victim ended up dead. Sometimes, perhaps, God didn't want the world to know that the victim was truly in-nocent. Or God let the real truth come out much later. Then the victim might become a recognized martyr or even a saint. Unlike torture by heathen Indians, civilized practitioners of 'Trial by Ordeal' or of valid Exorcism, had God on their side; therefore, Holy Mother, the Roman Catholic Church con-demned any exorcism under-taken without proper permission.

Bishop *Levele* had authorized *Friar Dominque Du Louches* to wrestle with *the Devil* and to cleanse Abel Freeman of pos-session by *Satan*, the adversary of Our Lord Jesus Christ. Oft' the *Dark One* might confuse witnesses of Exorcism. Despite such trickery *Levele* had ordered that *Du Louches* begin the severe examination and cleansing for all to see at High Noon, (the hour on the cross Christ was originally spiked).

The show began in the court-yard of *Chateau Frontenac,* in whose pantry-box basement Abel Freeman had been im-prisoned. Uniformed policemen on horseback went ahead to guarantee free movement for *Monk Du Louches, the Exorcist!* He wore the two-and-a-half foot high, pointed cap favored throughout the Spanish Inquisition. His head-gear was under-lined by a face-mask with cut out spaces for use of eyes, nose and mouth. Headdress and mask were of a white cancerous complexion like the Friar-Monk's cassock. Both habit and hat held a heavily-embroidered, black Gothic cross.

Du Louches had wanted a red Gothic cross; but *Levele* refused to approve the Friar's whim.

"Red was a color designated for a member of the clergy with the titular dignity of Monsignor or higher," reprimanded Bishop *Levele*. "Red relates to the blood of Canada's martyrs."

"But vestments with red sewing are worn by priests on some Sundays and Holy Days," argued *Du Louches*. "Even altar boys sometimes wear red cassocks!"

Levele was not swayed: "Red Dress might confuse the citizenry. They could wrongly believe that you were a Cardinal, for example." Then to temper the sting of humiliation, the Bishop said:

"You have the natural bearing of a Purple-&-Crimson robed Cardinal."

Pleased to recall his Excellency's insight, the dumpy, clownish-figured *Du Louches* emitted a stream of gaseous expulsions. And the parade-like march to the Upper Town's Cathedral was ready to begin. The route was lined with individuals and groups who considered themselves especially holy. Along the narrow streets the people were three deep. Anymore and they'd risk getting run over. Onlookers hung out from upper floor windows. The Exorcist nodded.

And a lay Brother, garbed in a bear-skin-fur hide (like a hermit reminiscent of St. John the Baptist) and carrying a Processional Crucifix, started to walk. The Seminary School's boys dressed in red cassocks and holding tall candles followed the Christ-Figure Bearer. Priests with swinging Censor and an Incense Holder shuffled after. They were like an Honor Guard.

Older and middle girls from the Ursuline Convent School came next, singing: *"Hallelujah!"* Younger girls carrying baskets proceeded to drop flower-petals along the roadway. *Du*

Louches, in his peaked-cap and peek-a-boo mask, pompously strode forward. Oh, how he longed for the days of *the Spanish Inquisition*, when some thirty prelates or more wearing towering conical hats dominated the ground. His own mask was part of a disguise to perplex *the Devil*. Priests, Monks and Brothers mingled together at the end of the pedestrian column. A big black horse rigged with high black plumes and festooned in black crepe pulled an old straw-strewn tumbril, in which slumped the blinded Abel Freeman. A squad of French Cavalry terminated the line.

More horse soldiers with swords and riot batons safeguarded the square. With them, the majority of remaining 'Religious' awaited in front of the Cathedral, where the Judgment Stand stood over the heads of the multitude. Most of the Ursuline Nuns were there in this rare public appearance; as they waited for their students, they sung hymns in praise of the Redeemer. The Bonfire foundation had been laid for those who had won their bid for the privilege of placing a piece of fire-wood into the purification flames. The rank and file of the participants-in-spirit numbered in the thousands. The normal activity of *the City* had been set aside for the trial.

Earlier, such as in Salem, Massachusetts (1692), where a Witch Hunt resulted in a score of suspects hanged, full community trials were conducted against congress with *the Devil*. *Du Louches* turned his neck around and glanced at the chained dupe in the tumbril. No *Voo Doo* was evident. But he had prepared a surprise, in case Abel Freeman were proven exorcised, but yet guilty. The Friar-Monk splurged a pooper and adjusted his clothed-in-black-velvet, iron-hand. In his belt he held a hard, leather-&-canvas paw to put on, if his regular, heavy iron-hand grew too heavy, as the day wore on.

Morning lazily meandered into afternoon at Beaver Lodge. Karen Bluejeans tracked down Lawrence Pena by the sound of a full grown goat's loud bleat from hilly bourn. He was with the herd of half-dozen streaked, speckled and grizzled goats (his proxy Alpaca, Llama and little Vicuna) that he had hidden.

"The animals aren't secure here anymore," the shepherd said. "Even *Paint* is allowed to remain here only as a stabled emergency steed," he related to the girl. "The army wants everything that moves. And even strangers come around looking for food to eat."

"Jack and I ate shellfish last night," she told him.

"You've got to stop feasting the prisoner," he replied. "You two orgy like you're decadent aristocrats in a declining Imperial Rome. The countryside is barren. People are starving."

"I want to go away," she said, her feelings slightly bruised because of how Pena had referred to Jack. "Can you provide us with a boat to cross over the river?"

"Does your father know? he questioned; "How will Jack leave? When do you plan to go?"

"I'm not sure," said Karen Bluejeans. "I need your help. Jack's gotta escape."

Lawrence Pena looked old and wise. He also looked fatigued. From the little foothill's foliage of Hazel, Maple and Birch trees, forever foreign to the jungle vegetation of his native Peru, he somberly stared past the dirt-fields devoid of crops and the enclosed-gardens empty of plants – out onto *the Plains of Abraham*, where the cliffs dropped down to the River. Like the mythical boatman *Charon*, or some other ancient ferryman, such as, perhaps, the gondolier in the Chinese Blue Willow story where a pair of young lovers change into birds and fly away, he said: "Yes. I can help with a boat for you to cross the river and escape to the other side."

CHAPTER VII.

B orn in *Eisleben*, near *Berlin* (1483), Martin Luther, a monk married to Katharina von Bora, translated the Bible into German and prescribed the common rendition for the German language. He was excommunicated from the Catholic Church for posting on *Wittenberg Castle's Church Door* his *Ninety-Five Theses* that emphasized papal abuse. Paramount protest apostatized *contre* "the selling of indulgences," for reduction of purgatorial punishment, and thus became the hard core of the Protestant Reformation.

Through the Sacrament of Penace, God in His Infinite Charity and Mercy forgives the sinner for spiritual transgression; but punishment is still due. An Act of Contrition might atone with the saying of a Rosary; or the penalty to pay back for an offense might consist of years and years of bondage. One could purchase an indulgence that should pay for a period of time in purgatory, the afterlife's place in between heaven and hell, where sins were bargained for in burning fires. However, the greatest punishment was being denied the Communion of God's Presence. Like purchased indulgences, prayers, almsgiving and fasting reduced punition.

Professional 'indulgence' salesmen could knock off years

of punishment in Purgatory for the right price. And many of the monetary payments went towards the construction of Cathedrals and Universities on Earth. Luther rebelled against the doctrine of 'selling indulgences'; instead, his theology offered a cheerful, personal rapport through Christ's grace, without the Papacy's middle-man deals. Salvation eventuated from 'justification by faith alone." The Pope in Rome condemned the outlaw Dissident who had disfranchised selling indulgences; Yet, five years after the Council of Trent, Pope Pius V dispensed altogether with the Selling of Indulgences (1562).

Martin Luther had been a Friar before becoming a Monk, but *Du Louches* had nothing else to compare with the major Founder of Protestantism on the Continent. Nor did *Dominique Du Louches* think it right to deny his Canada's congregation the opportunity to take an active hand in prosecuting *the Devil's* disciple (as well as, earning indulgences for remission of sin). Hence, he sold sticks of firewood or faggots that had been promised a position in the purging Bonfire. One bid at a pre-set price to pay for the piece of wood. *Joe Cadet* monitored the buying and selling. He split his profit with *Bigot*. Nonetheless, Joe saw to it that nobody got their rod until the last minute. For a provoked, club-armed crowd could turn on the establishment and the Excorcist. *Du Louches* laughed at Cadet's concern for the fuel-purchasing, vigilante visitors, farmers and townsfolk.

Du Louches laughed also when his farts sounded loudly, as they did now, as he mounted the steps up to the platform of the Judgment Stand. Abel Freeman had been dragged to the tall stake stuck in a (soon to be shape-shifting) pyramid of kindling and starter firewood and chained up. Dried blood darkened the pits that once were his eyes. He looked like a pathetic clown from "Commedia Dell 'Arte," [the Italian, 'comedy drama of the professional players' that acted before cathedrals]. *Du Louches* called out to him from the altar of justice. The mob roared.

From a window of the Cathedral's quire, Bishop *Levele* studied the scene below. His guest, Bigot was heartily laughing at these players: Abel Freeman, *Du Louches* and *Du Louches's retinue*; most of all *Bigot* enjoyed the riled up peoples:

"What characters!" exclaimed the *Intendant*. "Can you believe this oddity of individuals?"

"Anything to drink?" the *Intendant* asked. *Levele* did not reply. The Bishop was too busy bitterly realizing that Karen Bluejeans was not with the other girls of the Ursuline Nuns Convent School.

The leader of Ursuline Nuns had been unable to consider the Bishop's request to send the Mic-Mak girl to his Confessional. Nor could she speak to Karen Bluejeans. Retreat into prayer supervened.

Inside her private chapel, *Mother Superior Marie Etienne* lit two tall candles and entered the long, seventeen foot aisle of her *Prix Deux*. An additional foot might be calculated if the kneeler itself were counted. That should make eighteen, which was divisible by Three, a fixed, mystical sacred number representing *The Trinity*. The long aisle was carpeted with a gift from King Philip II of France (Philip Augustus), an Arabian Rug (or Runner) stolen or sacked from *Saladin* during the Crusades of the early Middle Ages (12th Century), when Christian Europe fought to take back Jerusalem and the Holy Land from Islam's Muslims.

No rosary did she bring, but rather a knot-braided rope. At the cushioned kneeler, she divested the upper parts of her habit. Bare-breasted, she fell to her knees and slapped the rope over the kneeler's prayer bar.

"Lord God, forgive us," she prayed. "Make my pain sweeten your suffering at *Golgotha*."

"Thud!" The rope wielded with both hands came down hard over her shoulder onto her back.

"Ah!" She cried loudly. She could not observe the rule of silence. The heavy knob at the end of her rope had hit an already vulnerable bruise, purplish black-&-blue. Contacting the tender area caused the skin to break. She bled there and began to feel faint and light-headed.

The fingers of her hands could barely grip to hold the rope, her arms trembled to flog down the whip onto her battered, bloodied backside. Her heart and lungs convulsed and felt like bursting. Weeping wet tears of despair and grief, she cried out:

"O Lord! Do not forsake me. Please, help your servant."

Again she raised the bludgeoning chord and struck:

"Thud!" Her back caved into a mushy pulp. And this time the hurt had exerted too much physical suffering. The middle-aged woman's body died of shock and the trauma of heart failure. Dead! *The Mother Superior Marie Etienne* slid down onto the floor, her prayer rug transforming into a pool of blood, her *Prix Deux* metamorphosing into her *Catafalque*.

"The spirit is willing, the flesh is weak."

Condemned, Abel Freeman, mouth agape, only imagined what was happening. The Exorcist, with exaggerated drama, the Exorcist climbed down the Judgment platform's ladder and rushed unto the possessed man. A member of the laity dressed like a Roman soldier had been positioned there that *Du Louches* might take up a lance and spear the black man:

"Did you see the way his head had been nod-bobbing?" he asked those close at hand. *"The Devil* was bearing false witness through him."

Du Louches jumped up and down throwing a little jig-like tantrum. He screamed:

"They were in contempt of court!"

A battalion of police now pushed back the angrily shouting, self-righteous throngs. The citizenry believed that the famine, plague and misfortunes that had befallen Canada should disappear in the thick black smoke arising from the eventual sacrificial fire of red, orange and yellow flames. After *the Devil's* darling was burnt in exorcism, – peace, prosperity, and purposeful existence should prevail. Well aware of their attitude, *Du Louches* pooped a series of really bad-smelling stinks, and he quickly reconsidered *Cadet's* earlier alarm. But this crowd might get out of hand even without firewood cudgels. In the clearing before the shackled, blind fiend, *Du Louches* gave the pre-agreed upon signal: arms outstretched like Jesus on the cross, he spun around and around like a twirling top. He was still wearing the yard-high, conical hat.

The Physician, wearing a bird-head's mask with a long pointy beak, stopped *Du Louches;* and from somewhere behind the Judgment Stage a string of pale-white, sulfur-yellow powdered Neophytes, costumed as Zombies, formed into a circle around the Exorcist. Actually, *Du Louches* desired to wear the Bird-Head mask, but it was reserved for the Physician; the beak contained pleasant spices that the Doctor might investigate open sores and other wounds or injuries without experiencing their possible malodorous particularity. The conical, Dunce-like Cap that *Du Louches* wore was designed to transmit 'Exorcist Thought', directly in supplication towards Heaven.

The hats, masks, dance and chanting *Voo Doo* figures were special effects to not only drive out *the Devil*, but also to appease the onlookers. For example, the face of each of the androgynous Zombie anatomies bore an unique mask: one wore black-face, another a Viennese eyes-masque, and many displayed kinky colors, dots, and lines in geometrical patterns. The children of *the Devil* crawled forth from the madness of corruption.

Voo Doo derives from *Vodun,* which means 'god' in the *Fon* language of *Benin*, Africa. The religion is practiced primarily in *Haiti,* and it ritualizes Serpent Worship and 'Necromancy' (or conjuring up spirits of the dead). *Kongo* was the name given to the *Voo Doo* snake god who entered the dead body to re-animated the soul of the deceased. *Du Louches* had kept his phony Zombie *Ioa* Corps in reserve to quell rioting, if his program should lose authority. However, now these ancestral angels of abomination were kneeling in submission to the Processional Crucifix while from his pole their *Boogie Man* bled. It was only a flesh wound, a superficial scratch. *Du Louches* had been careful not to kill his Black star attraction.

After the Exorcist had blessed them, the Physician with a forefinger touched each born-again-Christian, Zombie. They then stood up erect like men. 'That's it', thought *Du Louches*. Next time, we should have one big log placed before the Bonfire; the purchaser merely need touch the timber to symbolize his contribution. The way we're going to do it now will take forever. And the Friar was hungry. He emitted a loud cracking fart; and he didn't care if anybody heard it.

Nonetheless, *Cadet* began to marshal the line of faggot buyers into a single-file parade. One by one they handed their firewood stick to a big, lumberjack-like Brother who placed it onto the pile. Making artistic symmetry, his Zombie saints bunched into two choir sections on each side of the monster's pike. They cantillated songs akin to Gregorian Chant or Snake Charming. From the long line of buyers that twisted and turned, like a giant serpent slithering through the milling masses of human beings, *Du Louches* and the Physician stood off.

Surrounded by the masses the Exorcist pictured himself as a snared *Purple Martin* of the fields, unlikely to escape the snares of the fowler. He wanted to remount the Judgment Stand, but he felt too lazy to climb up the ladder. The crowd, however, was like a drunken giant awoken from a wine-induce slumber; and, therefore he must make a move. Buckets of grease and oils to make black smoke splashed onto the fire-wood, now set for ignition.

Du Louches had studied the lighting of her fire when the English burned France's national heroine *Saint Joan of Arc* alive, as a witch at *Rouen* (1431). After hearing heavenly voices (St. Michael, St. Catherine, St. Margaret), the nineteen-years-old peasant girl of *Doremy* field-marshaled *the Dauphin's* armies against invaders until she was captured; yet she had preserved *the Valois dynasty* with the coronation of *Charles VI* at *Reims*, a kind of turning point in the Hundred Years War. Historical texts indicated that at first the tinder would not catch, as though her God had sent cherubim to blow out the spark. But once the fire caught, the flames flamed up very prettily. *Jeanne d'Arc, of La Purcelle Orleans*, "*the Maid of Orleans*," expired in a radiant light of beauty. Her 'last word' was: "Jesus!" The Exorcist didn't expect as much from Abel Freeman. Just shovel the bum into a latrine as though he were defecation or pitchfork him back into *the Devil's* pit, burning black coals under red-&-white fire. *Du Louches's* anus spewed a stream of intestinal gas.

Nobody commented upon the offense. Whether believer or atheist, these persons were as sheep to the goodly Friar. And this termination of the *noir*-stained trespasser shalt remove doubt of disbelief in *the Devil*. No God or man should allow the pain, suffering and perdition delivered to Abel Freeman. *Du Louches* was handed the long, flame carrying torch, and told all.

"Let this fiery solemnization redeem the Boogie Man's sins."

And so saying, he tossed the fire-flake-flaring torch into the *centre* of the black man's funeral pyre. Crackling flames leaped around as though in a dance. The audience cheered, yelled and screamed hysterically.

"Kill the Christ hater!"

"Crucify him!"

"Burn him to Death!'

His swollen, water-parched tongue hung out of his mouth and his opaque-blemished eye spaces glared in dumbness. His bones sizzled out of joint and his heart melted like molten wax. The golden flames of purging fire immolated Freeman. A wind-pushed pillar of black smoke like a tornado ascended into the clouds. The blackened smut smeared the sky for miles.

"*Mxyrztl yesoplat! Mxyrztl yesoplat!*" shouted *Du Louches*. He held his arms outspread as though conjuring up a wild spirit. And his big butt burped a noisy, noisome stench.

In the Cathedral's choir chamber *Bigot* laughed and pulled a flask of brandy from his coat pocket. He took a gulp, and said:

"He got burnt!" Then, he candidly asked, "Was this guy really a Daemon?"

"I doubt it," said *Levele*. "But he kept the swine from getting underfoot, for a while."

Bigot laughed, again. And he took another pull of Brandy, again saying: "He got burnt!"

The Bishop left the loft and headed for the *Chateau Frontenac*. Like a hunter hunting at the last place that he had seen his prey, *Levele* was on the scent of a certain Karen Bluejeans. He sought a clue.

The slanting pillar of dense black smoke aroused curiosity. Chief Engineer Mackeller said that Captain John Knox at *Pointe Levi* with the artillery howitzers, had suggested that an ammunition depot must have accidentally blown up in the Upper Town. Aboard the brevet flagship, *Prince of Wales*, Wolfe nodded agreement while studying through his spyglass Quebec City's defenses along its eastern shoreline. Brigadier General Robert Monckton should land there in between *Beauport* and the adjacent *St. Charles River,* where it flowed into the St. Lawrence River, as a diversion from the main attack on *Levis* camp. Simultaneously, he [Wolfe] should cross *the Montmorency River* from the recently established British encampment to overpower the Second Redoubt in the French line of extended protection. Also, a Naval attack should occur, with troops transported from *Ile d'Orleans*, as well as more troops rafted across the St. Lawrence to the west of the 2nd Redoubt, the battle's major focus. The strategy hoped for *Montcalm* to aid *Levis* and to come out from the fortifications to fight on open ground.

On the British far left flank, between *Beauport* and Quebec City's suburbs of *St. Roch* and *Palais, the St. Charles* emptied; but now the main flow was blocked by chained-together logs and two sunken ships bristling with workable cannons. Farther back on a rise *Montcalm* commanded from a stone house surrounded by round white tents. Nearby above the log-boom were the stations of the famous 'let the mouth of my cannon reply' cannons; Quebec City boasted over 106 guns.

Centurion (three-mast frigate of sixty-four guns), defense hero of the French fire-ships attack, commanded the catamarans *Russell* and the *Three Sisters*, (14 guns each) laden with troops, into the zone near *the Montmorency* shore. The parallel hulls of the cats cradled more stability than a single keel. They were broad a-beam, like Cook's collier and years later *H.M.S. Beagle*, upon which, from Ecuador's *Galapagos Islands*, Charles Darwin researched the rudiments for the theory of evolution: *The Origin of Species by Natural Selection*. Under the *Centurion's* watchful eye, the twin hulls kept the cats afloat in shallows to pummeled enemy entrenchments on the north shore near *the Montmorency River*, in the stark hills above the splashing high-water-line; but the naval guns fell too low to cause substantial harm.

Meanwhile, Brigadier General George Townshend was to deploy at the head of 2,000 troops from the British Camp, beneath the 250 - 300 foot drop of *Montmorency Falls* on the eastern side of *the Montmorency River*. An artillery barrage of fifty cannons commenced his assault. The diversionary strike at *Beauport* was set aside; but Monckton had reinforcements for Townshend, including thousands and thousands of musket cartridges, two highly-maneuverable light cannons, and engineering/pioneering implements such as shovels, picks, axes and other tools that should help establish the British stronghold once it were created.

Wolfe believed that the 2nd Redoubt was situated in a location that was separate from the others on the line. Just enough distance measured there to evade the backlash of French musketry. It should become the outpost, from which, Wolfe's army could grapnel-hook a hold on the cliffs. *Montcalm* must crawl out of his hole and fight or risk overwhelming English penetration of the *Levis* campsite and then the Quebec City defenses.

As Brig. Gen. Murray (1,000 troops) arrived by boats to reinforce Brig. Townshend (2,000 troops), the catamarans ran aground. While the tide went down, the cats had got stuck in the thick mud. The original plan called for them to land their troops and then to serve as floating batteries and relay posts, but now like a stick in the mud the idea of working with them seemed non-utilitarian. General Wolfe took *the Sutherland's* jolly boat to scrutinize the situation up close and to determine if further attack was feasible.

The French gunners and sharpshooters racked the landing forces with fire. The *Macau* cane Jack had given to James was broken and splintered. Townshend's receding line was going to run into Murray's disembarking men, with a disorderly retreat like Braddock's fiasco in the making. General Wolfe was on the verge of signaling a strategic withdrawal when impatient for their share of fresh laurels Frasers Higlanders charged the 2nd Redoubt and took it, broadswords gleaming with wet blood.

Crossfire from higher up in the cliffs and rolling hills slaughtered the recent conquerors who couldn't close with a hand's holdfast or toe's foothold to climb higher. Then the clouds suddenly broke open the rain poured down relentlessly. In the slippery mud, sand and gravel the Highlanders met a cruel end. They contributed more than any regiment to the total of 434 dead.

Over the grim killing field upon an overgrown, brute white nag rode a giant skeleton in black-armor clad. A huge scythe dripping blood, he carried, like a sanguine banner of extinction. His upraised visor gleamed while exposing a grinning skull with cracked, gore-stained teeth. Death!

"Oomph! Oomph! Oomph! The muffled, muted horns sounded a mournful moan. They dragged out the living moment, yet:

"Death doth hath dominion!" Look! In the corner, ashy particles of sand run down in an hour-glass. The end has come.

Wolfe wrote to Pitt that the Navy was more than partially responsible for the Montmorency debacle. James Cook had sounded the waters and promised that the cats and bigger ships should sail closer to the shore than they actually had managed to do. Despondent, the General refused to contemplate returning to England less than victorious.

'Quebec City is not quite its old self', thought Karen Bluejeans, as she walked toward the jail. *Friar Du Louches's* Exorcism of *the Devil's* incarnation in Abel Freeman and *Marquis de Montcalm's* slaughter of the British Army at Montmorency yesterday, had created a nostalgic ambience in *the City's* streets, despite the debris and bombed out ruins. Her medicine pouch full of cocaine was tied around her neck underneath her mother's sparkling diamond necklace, which she wore to distract the guards. The twilight air was cool enough to wear a full-length, black Mink Coat. Beneath it she had stripped Indian fashion to a brassiere-like, dark scarf and beaded, leather loincloth that held an especially *petit* pistol and a Bleeding- Heart Tomahawk. Hard-toed Moccasins, and a Scalping Knife shived in a laced, thigh-high, deer-skin legging, armed her further.

Inside the coat, she had concealed two loaded Dueling Pistols and a Cutlass for Jack. And she carried a small picnic basket of sandwiches and jars of poisoned cider for the gaolers. Tiny pieces of shredded chicken had been packed for the lock-up's orange-striped cat, *Monsieur Circumflex*. With a glance she looked for the cat in the corner near the door to the cellar, as she stepped into the Jailer's Office.

"Hi!" she said, flamboyantly. "Anyone for chicken sandwiches and brown ale?"

The prison guards heartily approved. One of the three whistled in appreciation of the girl's evening attire, make-up and ratted hair, save for single braid. She exaggerated movements in her hips and torso. Laughter reverberated in the room. A guard very gentlemanly opened the door to the basement for her. Without hesitation she hurried down the steps to caged Jack Wales.

She opened the long Mink Coat and held onto the prison bars with outstretched arms. A wave of sensuous perfume emanated from her body. She pursed her lips a little to make an innocent look. Jack eagerly kissed her mouth.

She handed him the guns and then the cutlass, saying:

"I've got cocaine to make us stronger." She poured the white powder out into straight lines on the naval, boarding sword's broad edge. With a hollowed Loon bone they took turns sniffing up the cocaine into their blood stream. Then she said:

"Go lie down. I'll call the jailer."

Just as she was about to turn and head for the stairs, he grabbed her arm, pulled her close to him, and said:

"Karen Bluejeans you must remember. If something bad happens and I don't escape, you must get to General Wolfe and tell him about your secret passage. Tell him that I sent you with this message: 'Elephant -&- Castle, Queenside on the *Plain of Abraham*.'"

"What do you mean, – 'if something happens?'" she asked. "Why shouldn't you escape to give the message yourself?"

"I mean," replied Jack, if I should slip and break a leg or anything like that. You've got to go over the river tonight with the intelligence for Wolfe."

Karen Bluejeans sniffled. And her mascara ran a little, as tears moistened her eyelashes.

"Jack!" she said, "I don't want something bad to happen. Jack, I can't live without your love. I can't conceive of your death. Don't let anything bad happen."

"If worse comes to worst, we will meet again in another lifetime," Jack said, softly as he smoothed her hair with his fingertips. "Just don't neglect to inform Wolfe. Our whole world depends on delivering that knowledge of the secret pass."

"I'll try," she lisped. "Elephant-&-Castle on the Queen's side. On *the Plain of Abraham*."

Jack went to the bed and waived a dueling pistol toward the stairs. Karen Bluejeans ran up to the guardroom and called for help. She said that the prisoner was secreting liquids and vomiting. She thought that Jack was dying. Gruff *Yves* said that he'd have a look and followed the girl down the stairs.

"There!" cried Karen Bluejeans, almost hysterically pointing to the dark figure lying upon the cot. "He looks dead."

"Hold on, dearie," said *Yves*. He opened the cell door and walked in to inspect Jack's quiet form. "Hey, you," he barked at Jack, as he shook the silent one's shoulder.

"Hey, yourself," said Jack, suddenly reaching up and yanking *Yves* by the collar into the fist of brass knuckles made by his cutlass's grip. Gruff *Yves* was knocked out cold.

"Come on!" hurried, Karen Bluejeans. Jack took keys and weapons, when the jailer not only regained consciousness, but also wrestled Jack into the bunk and down onto the ground.

"What going on here?" shouted the other guard who had descended the stairs. He rushed toward the cell's open gate. Karen Bluejeans stepped in front of him. He swung at her jaw with the butt of his musket. She blocked his weapon with her tomahawk.

The Mic-Mak teen hissed and spit in the face of her opponent. He tried to overpower her with his firearm, but she slid her hatchet-like defense along the barrel of his weapon, spun and with a side swing into his eardrum area and spiked open his skull. Blood spurted out and splattered all over everywhere. The pointed end of her battle-axe drooled blood down its blood-gutters into the bleeding-heart cutaway, which now was soaked and sticky with her adversary's life fluids.

Without thinking twice she stabbed him with her knife.

"Stop!" commanded the third guard. He stood in the doorway looking at the female warrior, blood-dripping toma-hawk in her left hand, scalping knife draining drops of blood in her right hand. She had shed her blood-smeared fur coat and was appearing pretty athletic. The jail- keeper held a sort of shot-gun. He aimed at her, but both Ortiz and *Golden Bear* had trained her with knife. She dropped down onto one knee while throwing her blade directly into the man's chest, around the region of the heart. His gun went off high into the ceiling. As he fell down Karen Bluejeans ran to him, kicked him in his groin, and with both of her hands holding her tomahawk, sunk the weapon into his forehead to split open his skull, right between the eyes.

Worked up, she retrieved her knife and ripped up the dead man's hair to scalp him. Holding the knife savagely high over her own head, she was ready to make a war whoop, when Jack suddenly stayed her forearm.

"Come on, Red! We don't have time for all that," he said.

She jumped into his arms and they kissed, blood and per-spiration streaming down her neck and breasts, and through her underarm hair, and her midriff, her lower back, her crotch, inner thighs and calves, sweat and blood trickling down the crack between the cheeks of her rear end and her tall hind legs. Her tongue and lips tasted like blood. She was all blood; and in the bloody process she had felt involuntary orgasm, also.

Jack was without stain until they had embraced. He and *Yves* had fought like big boys in a schoolyard, until Jack finally got an upper hand. Wales broke gruff *Yves*'s neck. Now the Royal Marine Officer focused from experience.

"One shot got off. Somebody might have heard it," he reasoned, as he wiped blood and released fluids from the body of his girlfriend. "We've got to go."

"Come on," she said, taking his hand as she started up the stairs: "I've seen some overcoats hanging up in the guardroom.

At the top of the stairs *Circumflex* stood broadside to look big. Seeing her, he rubbed against her leg and meowed: "Hello."

"Oh, Jack. Let's take *Circumflex*. He's been with us, almost from the beginning," she said, picking up the striped creature. "Yes?"

Jack helped her put on an old uniform overcoat. And he put on a prison-guard coat. As she stepped to the door; the cat cradle like a baby in her arms, meowed: "Me."

"Karen Bluejeans won't abandon you, *Monsieur*," she whispered while hugging the cat; but the French-brought-up cat struggled out of her arms. He jumped up onto the table where remnants of the chicken sandwiches remained.

"Let's go!" said, Jack stepping between the girl and her return into the room for the cat. "He has his own destiny. We've got to go."

"Au revoir, Mon petit!" Karen Bluejeans bubbled. ['Goodbye, my little one.]

"Hurry," said Jack, pushing her out the door. Their moods were remarkably playful considering the horrendous escape they had been through, and the three dead men left down in the cellar. Jack's non-concern might be attributed to his rank in the Royal Marines; whereas, Karen Bluejeans only appeared concerned that she had fought for her man, and she seemed unaware of the moral objections and consequences capable of arising from her barbaric actions. They moved out into the courtyard beneath cloudy night skies.

Meanwhile, the Bishop *Levele* had been busy. Upon confirmation of Mother Superior *Marie Etienne's* death, he renewed his search for Karen Bluejeans. He only permitted the momentary interruption of transferring *Du Louches* to *Montreal*. Disgusted at the sight of the fat, pompous and sanctimonious Friar, *Levele* tightened the drag-net for the Indian girl. When told that she had gone back to the dungeon, he bee-lined there to find the escaping Lovers.

Jack wore a guard's overcoat with a *tuques* (knit or sock cap). Karen Bluejeans resembled a a Polish Drum Major wearing a coat with tails, red lapels and a four-inch wide Sergeant's Chevron; a broad Napoleonic-like hat with an Ostrich Feather made her stand out as one of the elite Palace Guard, except for the blood smeared on her face like daubed war paint. Jack blended into the background, but the girl demanded attention. *Levele* guessed what had happened. He sounded the alarm:

"Help! Murder! The prisoner has escaped! The pirate is at large! Help!"

Surprisingly several soldiers carrying muskets approached.

"There!" cried *Levele*. He pointed to the two escapees who were climbing up the wall to the rampart walkway. This was their shortest route of escape. They had talked about which way to go after leaving the cellar. The western route through *the St. Louis Gate* and across *the Plain of Abraham* to the river was too risky. The secret passage might become too protected for Wolfe to traverse later. The eastern direction towards *Beauport* was crowded, but they might have the opportunity to slip through undetected. Anyway that is where Pena had put their boat, a beat-up, old canoe-like rowboat.

Atop the palisade Jack crouched and fired one of the

dueling pistols. A soldier fell dead. Two, no three shots retaliated. Jack fell against the wall. Karen Bluejeans had lost her cap. She held Jack up with her arms under his. More shots plucked away at Major Wales's torso. He bled from the chest and stomach in several places. She fell onto her left knee and supported the shrinking body of her lover over her right knee. Her pain and empathy for Jack's suffering was comparable perhaps to the Virgin's at the foot of the Cross, her acceptance of Christ's sacrifice for the Redemption of Mankind. A sword of sorrow was stabbed into her heart. And Jack died.

She kissed him one last long kiss on the mouth. Her tears tasted like salt. His body was small now like a little child's. She put him down into a puddle of his own blood. Soldiers were now on the palisade. *Levele* was screaming, like a farm woman chasing a fox away from the henhouse.

"Catch her! Don't let her away! Get her!"

Standing up, she swung her leg over the wall like climbing onto her pony. But she kept her profile low. Bullets whistled after her. Into the darkness she fell about twenty-one feet. Shouts and yelling sounded on Jack's side of the wall. She stood up and ran in between shrubbery bushes, repeating in her mind:

"Elephant-&-Castle! Elephant-&-Castle! Elephant-&-Castle!:

Karen Bluejeans rushed into the night, the river mists and historical legend.

Josef the Woodcutter carefully placed his feet along the margin of the cluttered stairwell at *Holy Child Chapel.* Ignoring the British howitzer shells being shot from *Pointe Levis,* he had come to talk with his wife, *Marie.* A candle lent its light into the gray gloom of the underground, where the caskets, coffins, and tombs of the dead rested. *Marie's* sarcophagus was beneath the altar, a place of honor.

Josef pressed against the stone panel with both arms open,

as though trying to embrace her through the hard mineral surface. His head hung on his arm in dejection. Then one hand was placed on the cover of the internment box. He pulled his chin up sort of like a puppy to rest atop the carrier also, and said:

"I miss you." He picked the candle up from the floor and melted some wax on the lid of the sarcophagus that the taper should stand upright.

"I'm lonely without you," he continued: "I'm not sure if you feel the same. Do the deceased realize loneliness? Or are you there in God's good heaven, with happy Saints and Angels like a brightly-colored holiday calendar?"

The building shook a little as though a small earthquake tremor had occurred. Dust and fine pieces of powder-like essences fell from the ceiling.

"That's your English bombing," he informed her. "Your Shakespeare people: *'To be or not to be?'*" He put his face into the crook of his elbow and wept. Straightening up, he wiped his eyes, and said:

"I don't know why I outlived you who were always so good to everybody and so full of life?" He rubbed his hand along the edge of her tomb like a carpenter feeling a freshly sanded piece of furniture, and related:

"Karen Bluejeans has taken a fancy to an Englishman. She's with him right now. Oh, he's an officer and a gentleman. She supports him. They plan to marry after the war is over." The foundations of *Holy Child Chapel* shook again. The candle's flames blew out.

Then as though lightning had been flung down from the cloudy firmament, a mammoth thirteen-inch shell crashed through the roof above. Without reducing momentum the projectile caved in the floor of the Sanctuary. Josef's oaken iconography, *God, the Benevolent Creator*, got swallowed up by the bomb-hole in front of the altar. Graves disgorged their corpses.

Marie's coffin arose upright spilling her dead body out as her sepulcher, which had split asunder to crush Josef. His creations and all of *Holy Chapel Child* burned from the explosive fires like a brightly lit Christmas Tree. The old *Habitant's* death was as appropriately symbolic of Quebec's disintegration within New France as a Canadian Maple tree being hewn to make room for a fresh settlement: "*The old Order changeth and giveth way to the new.*"

CHAPTER VIII.

*M*arquis de Montcalm cautioned his staff against *hubris* even though *the Battle for Beaufort* had been a victory. He now strategized to avoid further fighting and to prolong the siege until the enemy exhausted its supplies or the Canadian Winter came to scoot away the British. With some good luck for the *Marquis*, *Wolfe* would be retreating, dragging his tail behind him. Although *Vaudreuil*, *Bigot* and others (including Karen Bluejeans) had plenty to eat, most of the people in Quebec City survived on only two ounces of bread for each person per day. The 'will to go on' was bolstered earlier in the Spring, when through the British blockade, two French frigates successfully escorted a convoy of fourteen supply ships from France. *The Marquis's* greater concern than starvation was news of the oncoming Major General Amherst marching against Fort Ticonderoga, and from there on to *Montreal* and Quebec.

In the light of the wee hours of the morning's wanly moon, Lieutenant Jeremy Osborn stood on the quarter-deck of flagship Sutherland retelling his immediate subordinate the information just transmitted:

"Tomorrow night Wolfe will lead the Army across the river

to a secret landing place. Rumor hinted that only last night he had had a vision or he had been visited by a ghost who had flown over the icy river waters to report a hidden location."

"She is the daughter of *Donnaconan*, the local Indian chief, or allegedly, the Spirit of the River, itself," -- replied, the Duty Officer to Osborn. Now Jeremy's chance to retire as an innkeeper on the Isle of Wight seemed truly possible. Most modern sieges ended with victory by the hand of a turncoat; and now suddenly to guide them they had the River-Chief's Daughter!

Wolfe, Monckton and Mackellar had already surveyed the site through their spyglasses from *Pointe Levi,* which was approximately opposite the forgotten canoe-post called *Anse au Foulon.* They and others were now inside the Captain's Cabin, where Wolfe spoke to this high command:

"*The Marquis* is well aware that his forces are superior only in number. They will not hold up against us in an open European-style battle."

Brigadier General Monckton and Chief Engineer Major Mackeller presented bombardment statistics: Approximately, 6,000 projectiles had been hurled against *the City*: 2,326 13-inch shells, 1,588 10-inch shells, 1,600 cannon-balls, 300 disease and explosives-stuft carcasses, and 125 10-inch bomb conglomerations of deadly detonating metals and hurting things. Also, the General's ongoing campaign to cruelly ravage and devastate the countryside continued: up to 1,400 farms, along with sloops, schooners, and other bateaux, fishing vessels and small craft had been destroyed. Still, Vice-Admiral Sir Charles Saunders and Vice-Admiral Charles Holmes could not emphasize enough the opinion of First Lord of the Admiralty Anson that for the safety of the Royal Navy, the fear of a freezing St. Lawrence seaway prompted immediate action to storm Quebec City.

The St. Lawrence froze in two different ways. Below freezing temperatures (0' Celsius), along with freezing wind-chill factors (32' F), froze the water along the shoreline. Thick-furred wildlife-like beaver, otter and seals still had some access to their watery highway, until ice formed slowly out into the middle of the River. The other method was the deep freeze. Ice began to form on the River's bottom to freeze the warmer stratifications of water above the lower layers of ice packs. And although the middle of the River rarely froze, there existed the risk that massive cracking ice could crush a big ship, as though 't were as fragile as a toy sailboat that a child might sail amidst a pair of swimming swans and a flock of floating ducks on the ripples of a park pond. The ships and their seamen should be vulnerable to Indian attacks over the ice, too.

The Navy was ordered to run up and down the North Shore in an attempt to confuse the enemy. Every ninety minutes it seemed as though the British would deliver a landing party. Troops were to be boarded onto the ships and transports. Wolfe gave the general plan of attack but he reserved vital information for the actual occurrence.

Admiral Holmes delivered a deserter, a Canadian traitor, found with a big sack of flour on his back while trying to ford the waters. Taken before the assembly of officers, Monckton, for Wolfe, questioned him:

"Well, what have you to say?"

"You'll all die," he out-cried: "Canada will prove the grave of the whole lot of you!"

"Imprison this foolish soothsayer and sneaky trader of ill tidings," interjected Townshend, who was the Godson of King George I. He loathed America's barbarity, he missed Charlotte, his wife, and he despised the prediction of the caught thief. Nobody countermanded his order.

The General's complexion was pale green due to his illness and laudanum medication. He retired with the Commander of the sloop *Porcupine*, his old school friend John Jervis [later Earl St. Vincent] to prepare his Will and Last Testament. The mini portrait of Catherine Lowther (afterwards the Duchess of Bolton) now surrounded by precious stones was put into the care of Jervis to return to her if he should meet *Nemeses*. Other personal items were designated. Wolfe summoned his orderly to unwrap a new uniform that he had purchased in Portsmouth.

On one hand, Sir Charles sailed *the Sutherland* and a group of escort ships as a diversion to *Beauport,* where stray, single-shot shelling of the shore set about. On the other hand, Vice- Admiral Holmes steadied the helm for the remainder of the British fleet that was beginning to congregate up river, past the guns of *Cape Diamond*. Around 3,500 troops were aboard ships and special transports, and another 2000 prepared to disembark from *Ile d' Orleans* and *Pointe Levis*. The exact landing cite had not yet been pinpointed by the General.

From out of the mildly overcast clouds a hunchbacked moon crawled out of the sky. As *Quasimodo* might have clung to a gargoyle along the battlements of *Notre Dame Cathedral of Paris*, so the lunar body hung for a moment above the events about to happen below, before lunging into the cloudiness. No substantial light shone to give away the surprise attack.

At 2PM the tide ebbed and with a fresh wind, Saunders aboard *the Sutherland* sent two lanterns up the mainmast's rigging, as a sign that the invasion had begun. And for two hours the whale-boat-like transports traversed the St. Lawrence River to their destination, the little cove: *Anse du Foulon*! Several officers sitting in one of the leading boats with the General Wolfe remembered that he had softly recited parts of Thomas Gray's *Elegy Written in a Country Churchyard*. Having experienced a perceptibility of death, the General Wolfe commented that he should rather have written those lines than taken Quebec. Of special note, he felt:

".. The boast of heraldry, the pomp of pow'r, And all the beauty, all that wealth e'er gave,

Awaits alike th' inevitable hour:

The paths of glory lead but to the grave. ."

"The paths of glory lead but to the grave." Thomas Gray (1716-1771) whose *Elegy* had impressed Wolfe was born in London and educated at Eton with Horace Walpole (future Prime Minister). And although not prolific, he was the foremost literary figure of English Letters or Literature in the mid-18th century. He was alive and writing, a forerunner of the Romantic Movement, when Wolfe did wrestle for Quebec (1759). Gray died in Cambridge and was later buried in the country churchyard of his poem.

A captured French prize, now the British sloop *Hunter* (10 guns) heard the silence interrupted by a Gallic Sentinel calling out to the boats: "Who goes there?"

The French expected a provisions convoy from up river; but the supplies had been delayed; and Quebec City had not been informed of the protraction. A Highlander who had served in Holland and spoke perfect French replied to the query: "France!"

And when the sentry inquired of the regiment's name, he said:

"The Queen's. Victuals and equipment!"

Silence bespoke the foreboding doom of New France's downfall.

The boats flowed with the current without giving more of a specific password. The convoy had been much awaited for, since food and all sorts of supplies were practically non-existent.

And there were not any pack animals to transport means over the muddy roads. The French sentries wanted this delivery by river smooth and uninterrupted, which worked well for the British invader.

Captain Knox later wrote in his journal that problems weren't encountered until the recess was arrived at, when an officer, soldiers and sailors were picked off and killed by French soldiers firing muskets at the approaching longboats. The *Guyenne Regiment* had set up a small camp at the foot of the narrow passage.

Formed in *Bordeaux,* 1st Battalion was retained for coastal duties in France, while 2nd Battalion of the *Bearn Guyenne* fought in New France. *The Regiment de Guyenne* (1755-1760), (white uniforms, red cuffs and pewter buttons) originally held jurisdiction over the private passageway and its hidden cove, as well as everything within three miles of *the Citadel's* western wall, including the *Plain of Abraham*, the *Sainte Foy* Road, Beaver Lodge and so on. But the *Montmorency* plucking of British feathers called for a new juxtaposition of the defenses. Quarters for the *Beam de Guyenne* moved closer to the *St. Charles*, where they could assist more efficiently against an attack on *Beauport*; Saunders had committed assault and battery in that area all night as a diversion to the actual landing at *Anse Au Foulon*..

Captain Louis Dupont du Chambon de Vergor (1713-1775) at 46 years old, accepted command, through *Bigot*, to defend the *Ansu Au Foulon*, which was rumored to not need more than a few good men with a couple barrels of rocks. *Montcalm* ascertained that 100 men might defend the location forever. *Vergor*, the loser to Monckton at Fort *Beausejour* (1755), now ruled the pass with the help of a few dozen men, the remainder of the original *Guyenne* guardians.

At 4: AM, Colonel William Howe, at the head of 24 volunteers stabbed bayonets into the loose rock to scale the heights about 200 yards from the cove. They then crept behind the pathway to take the cliff from its backside. Later, a horse, captured from the cliff-top's security post, was offered to the Major General; but Wolfe declined the bald, Bay mount in order to stand musket-in-hand, and shoulder to shoulder with his men, in the first of the two, thin Red Lines being drawn upon the *Plains of Abraham*.

George Lord Howe had created the Light Infantry or Flanking Infantry, as a counterpoint to French-&-Indian tactics. Uniforms were cut for frontier warfare and hair was kept short at two-and-one-half inches. Rocks, trees, stumps and other natural features of the terrain were incorpo-rated into their fighting. Wolfe considered Howe the best Officer ever in the British Army in North America. A fatal casualty at Ticonderoga, he was the elder brother in the family that included Admiral Richard, Lord Howe and also Lieutenant Colonel William Howe (later Major General William Howe, whose fame was won against the Americans at the victory of Bunker Hill, where the dead British soldiery mortally reposed strewn in the grass and yellow weeds of the battlefield, like fallen autumnal leaves).

Mark Cronath led away the Bay mount to General Monckton who had had command of the landing. He imme-diately lifted onto the steed, with his own orderly close at hand. Officers usually rode on horseback for mobility: to control ground, correct mistakes and to direct troops. both through the delivery of communiqués and also as a physical guidepost. Therefore, when General Wolfe deferred the brown horse to instead fight beside his men, he manifested inchoative dem-ocratic thought not unlike that of the ancient Greeks, pitted against Persia's tyranny of the battle-goaded, golden hordes of Asia, on *the Plains of Marathon*.

The Iroquois Confederacy was the only democracy apparent along the frontier, however; and Wolfe despised savages. Nevertheless, dismounted he continued making his warrior fraternity, a brotherhood of equality that he had initiated at the rallying concert. On equal footing at the far right, where traditionally the best Redcoats aligned, Wolfe presented himself as a target to enemy sharpshooters; but he was much less of a Bull's Eye than if he were riding a horse. He wore the head of his shattered cane affixed to a belt loop, but he did not wear the new uniform, which he had acquired for the decisive battle.

James Wolfe was of the old school that didn't owe undying devotion to any Regiment. Wolfe related to a clique like the Mafia whose business, social and military associations dominated hierarchal position; such a complex phased out when more professional indoctrination and training entered among the officer corps. Wolfe, himself, at fifteen served underage as an Ensign on the Army List. Thirty-three years old on the heights he was aware that all three waves of his approximately 4,000 troops had landed safely. Also some hard-nosed marines had lugged up two brass cannons, six-pounders: *Queen Elizabeth I* or *Lizzie* and *Milton* (the organ-pipes of English poetry). Prussia's Frederick had proven the deadly and crippling effect of even very small cannons of only two or three foot length; small cannonballs under 2 ½ pounds or grape-shot fired from the first few ranks had demonstrated devastating destruction.

The Major General had ordered his Adjutant General Issac Barre to temporarily halt the landing of troops after the First Wave; but Barre using self-initiative kept landing forces to avoid congestion at the cove. Division of troops might have been fatal for the British, just as Braddock's forces collided into one another; and Wolfe's earlier breaking of the Army into three groupings (at *Montmorency, Ile d'Orleans* and *Point Levis*) had been potentially dangerous, -- if the French should have enforced the axiom: "Divide and Conquer!"

But the Brits stayed united, just as first hint of day like a burning ember on the horizon glimmered. Fraser leading his Highlanders up the overrun *Guyenne* pass shook hands with Howe who was coming down from above, like the Word of God. Higlanders wore both the great and the little kilts (*feile-adh mor* & *feileadh beag*) with *the sett*. Along with regularly issued weapons, they carried the basket-hilted broadsword. Howe took them up to the top of the pass, the extreme end point of the *Cote d'Abraham* that led over on down to *the St. Charles River*.

When Howe and the 24 volunteers had followed scout Mark Cronath up the cliff's side, they snuck around behind the sentry outpost. There were two wooden houses, a stable and several tents set up. A Bay was half-saddled; her bridle and blanket were on. A Sergeant with his coat unbuttoned was sitting in the doorway of some straw tent smoking a clay pipe. Cronath ran up and flung his tomahawk into the soldier's *solar plexus*. Blood gushed forth like water from a fire-pump hose.

Some skirmishing ensued; but since Howe and his men had caught the French by surprise, there wasn't much in depth fighting. Yet no prisoners were taken, except *Vergor*, whom a volunteer had shot in the heel, sort of like an arrow into the weak spot of *Achilles*. But *Vergor* had had time to dispatch a messenger to *Montcalm* and another to *Bougainville*. Howe led a squad of six soldiers toward the Pass. Another quick skirmish occurred. It was then that Howe and Fraser shook hands:

"Kings of England and Kings of Scotland!" said Howe, somewhat school-boyishly.

Meanwhile, Mark Cronath found some more horses. And a scattered infiltration began of the area to the rear of *the Pathway's* opening, for fear that from here to *Cap Rouge* and *Montreal* another front might open.

Indeed, *Louis-Antoine Comte De Bougainville* (1729-1811) would ride at the head of 200 thronging cavalry. Behind him should march a little more than 2,000 infantry; and all along the way from *Cap Rouge* more armed personnel were going to be collected. In fact, this delay caused by the enlistment of individuals and small units most likely contributed to *Bougainville's* ultimate untimely arrival.

However, Corporal *Jules, Vergor's* messenger could not ride away on the great Bay that stood partially saddled at the outpost headquarters. The British were already everywhere running rampant. An alternative plan was taken. Across *St. Foy* Road, Beaver Lodge kept an extremely fast pony ready for message delivery. *Jules* rousted Pena the Lodge's caretaker to saddle up the steed. Within fifteen minutes *Paint,* the Pinto pony was prepared to carry *Jules* and the desperate note for immediate assistance to Bougainville. The French rider and his spotted pony took the very private back road, the Indian trail to the village of *Above the Falls*.

The fork split downwards to *the Cap* and the island stronghold of *Montreal*. *Bougainville* should have plenty of time to drive his army against the British landing at *Anse Au Foulon*. 'Undoubtedly, *Montcalm* will hold the English', thought Corporal *Jules*, 'the *Plain of Abraham* shall serve as an anvil, while *Bougainville* strikes like a hammer. Wolfe would be caught in between the two French-speaking forces and decimated!' The Pinto pony got a little hard to handle as the noise of the water and the scent of the water and the taste of the water in the air warned of the approaching Falls.

Pinto Pony received its name from the Spanish Jew, for --
'colorful' or 'painted'. The Portuguese in India interpret the
Pinto as 'mottled', a lively or restless individual. *Paint* was a
blue-eyed white horse with a pink muzzle, a black mane, black
stockings and a black tail; but the beast's coat color or spots
were patches of brown or Sienna; hence, he was a *Skewbald
Pinto*. Black spots should make him a *Piebald Pinto*. All color
patterning is genetic. Human beings compared to the Pinto are
called *partially Albino*. The Cream-&-Sienna running horse-
pony reared up at the sight of the rickety bridge across the
gorge of the waterfalls.

Jules struggled with the pony. He manhandled the creature
and yet the carrier only took a few forced steps forward. The
rider whipped the animal and dug his spurs into the pony's
flanks, producing blood-letting gashes. The messenger moved
to the middle of the bridge, where amidst the tumultuous
crashing waters and clouds of moist vapors, *Paint* reared up
one more time. His hooves clattered on the narrow bridge's
old planks. His hind hooves pounded over a ton of violent
pounding power. *Jules* used the whip to beat the horse-like
pony into submission, but to no avail. *Paint* struggled to keep
his balance, and he tripped. He fell. And the bridge collapsed.
The rider rode the pony plummeting to sure death on the
rapid-rife waters below. The bridge ends swung back and forth
in furious oscillations. *Bougainville* was within a matter of
minutes away, as the rosy-fingered dawn intermingled with
morning's pale grey light.

Across the bridges of *the St. Charles* at *Montcalm's* headquarters, *Vergor's* other messenger reported the disastrous de-
velopments of the British landing to *the Marquis*. *The Marquis*
could not believe his ears. Yet he wrote a quick note requiring
Bougainville to attack at once; the messenger dashed away

with the command. Then *Montcalm* called to saddle his own warhorse of destiny, *Montparnasse.* He issued general orders while dressing in white pants, a lacy white shirt and an antiquated breast shield beneath a dark blue coat adorned with medals; black riding boots & silver spurs, a gold-ribboned Black Tricorn and sword completed his ensemble.

His first look at the field came on horseback. *Montparnasse* was a heavy *Percheron*, the descendant of Arabians brought to *La Perche* in the south of *Normandy,* after victory over the Moors by *Charles Martel* (752 AD); from atop a small rise just beyond *the St. Charles*, *Montcalm* observed that he British had lined up in two long, thin ranks about a kilometer (a little more than a mile) away. Including flanking units the British force appeared around 2,500 strong. His own army assembled in an array of five major units, totaling over 6,000 men.

On the French Far Right: *La Sarre* (1685), white uniforms (with red, white or blue cuffs) and Black Tricorn with gold or white trim; *Mr. de Sennezerques* commanding; and at their side -- *Lanquedoc* (1672, by Louis XIV); the *Bearn Guyenne* in the Middle; *Royal Roussillon* (from *Languedoc-Roussillon* in Southeast France (with its *Catalan* painted wooden statues of the *Virgin and Child, Perpignon's* palm trees and bullfights in *Nimes*); and on the Far Left, *Montreal* and *Trois Rivieres* militias. Canadian sharpshooters and Indians fringed the flanks. Except for the Canadian militia and red men, the soldiers were French regulars.

Their adversary, on the British Far Right, stood the Light Grenadiers and 28th Foot (Royal Gloucestshire, Berkshire and Wiltshire Regiment); aside them the 43 Foot (Oxfordshire and Buckinghamshire Light Infantry/ the Royal Green Jackets); the 47th Foot (the North Lancashire Regiment, & the Queen's Lancashire Regiment). On the Far Left and backing as the second line held the 15th Foot (the East Yorkshire Regiment, the Prince of Wales's Own Regiment). Other Regiments filled in and guarded the flanks. The 35th Foot (the Princess of Wales's Own Royal Regiment) supported the Louisbourg Grenadiers. The 78th Foot, (Frasers Highlanders) kept a close eye on Wolfe who moved everywhere, especially to the right of the field.

The British Army's main front faced the amassed French soldiery; but the English also maintained a rearguard to protect against *Bougainville,* and a flanking front under Townshend to deflect encroachment by French skirmishers along the *St. Foy* Road. The right flank ran into the dizzying cliffs and the cold St. Lawrence River. The moist overcast sky sprinkled on and off lightly.

The sun occasionally made a partial appearance from behind clouds, as *Montcalm* rode before the ranks of his troops waving his sword. His men cheered. *The Marquis* had led them to victory up to this point; and they figured that there was no reason that the outnumbered British should finagle the prize now. The *Marquis de Montcalm* thought otherwise. He had realized that there wasn't an army in the world that could match this British Army of Wolfe's in an open European style battle. 1,500 troops protected *Beauport*. Where was *Bougainville?*

Louis-Antoine Comte de Bougainville never received the order to attack. *Montcalm's* courier had been picked off racing up the *St. Foy* Road. Mark Cronath, himself, had delivered the shot, killing *the Marquis 's* cry for help. Two alternatives existed. Quebec City could fall back and prepare for a siege; or the French forces (altogether around Quebec City about 14,000 men) could attack. *Montcalm* chose the latter, primarily because the British had already brought up two cannons; and next, they'd begin digging in for a European-like siege attack. Such an offense usually ended when the invaders breached the wall of the defending establishment. He ordered a steady advance of the regiments that were now close to only 2,500 meters (around 3,000 yards) away from the British front line.

Canadians and Indians sharp-shooted from the sidelines. And many a British soldier fell dead or wounded. Townshend countered with light infantry moving up into the gap between the two armies. This measure succeeded in diminishing the enemy snipers. Imperial Roman armies often put hundreds of impressed men or volunteers of foreign extraction into the fore of battle to weaken and confuse the opposition not greatly unlike the light infantry had worked here.

Lizzie (the brass six-pounder) boldly freewheeled up to spit out canisters of iron pellets into the main body of the French, who were still some six-hundred yards away. The cannon-fire was unwelcomed. The French assault fell apart.

Montcalm watched from a small knoll as the even march of his forces broke into pieces. The Right had slowed down, and the Center with the *Guyenne* (eager to win back their honor after losing the *Anse Au Foulon*) hurried ahead; and the Left (trying to keep up with the Middle) began to run. They fired at the British from a great distance. A couple Canadian Militiamen shot up into the air like Wild West Cowboys. Even when shots struck the enemy the harm done was null. One musket-ball hit a Highlander in the chest, but the velocity was already spent. 'Twas as though the kilted soldier wore a bullet-proof vest.

Most disruptive to the French open field attack though was the Canadian habit of lying down on the ground to reload. After firing, the Canadian would throw himself onto the ground, roll over onto his back and reload his weapon. This procedure like the later American Revolution tactic of hiding behind rock, tree or tree stump, reduced vulnerability to Redcoat weaponry; but here on *the Plain of Abraham* in the heat of the first European-style battle of North America, the falling down re-loaders tripped up the French regulars. All order and precision got knocked out of alignment. At one point, six or seven men piled up in a heap on top of one another like a clown act in a circus. Second in command, *La Sarre's General De Senezergues* died from light infantry fire.

Wolfe had his men lie down face first to subtract from the chances of their being killed or wounded by French gunfire. A Private from the front ranked 43rd Foot wrote in his daily journal that he remembers a long earthworm, red and juicy-looking, burrowing into the ground before him; the whole earth world wide was turned over by the ilk of such an entity. Another Private, this one from the 47th Foot noted that as he hugged the grassy earth he reflected upon his new sweetheart left behind in Portsmouth. And a Corporal of the 15th Foot (Prince of Wales's Own) in the back up line recalled: [paraphrased]

"I forgot where I was and what was happening, until suddenly *Milton* (the brass 'Lion of War' held in reserve and ready to unleash against any threat on the Western Front) went off roaring an invective that hurled an explosive into the forthcoming French mob. The explosion heaved up the ground, spurting dirt and distress cries into the sky like the upshot particles of a whale's waterspout!"

Montcalm had requested artillery to fight fire with fire; but *Lt. Gen. Ramezay*, the Acting Mayor and Military Governor of Quebec City provided only three cannons of the fortress' twenty-five pieces. He didn't want to be caught without them. And also, *Governor Vaudreuil* desired the defense artillery to remain inside the walls of *the City*. The three field guns were being positioned when it was discovered that the wrong gauge of ammunition had been brought along with them.

Without the aid of ordnance the French line like an unruly riot haphazardly stumbled on: the Left (comprised of the *Montreal* and *Trois Rivieres Militia* and *the Royal Roussillon Regiment*) came forward, as if their anger and erratic speed should protect against British arms; the *Bearn Guyenne* who had originally broken ranks continued to disorganize the attack; and the anchor unit, *La Sarre* no longer advanced in even lines at a steady pace. They had succumbed to the influence of the others and more or less marched in double-time or lagged behind. *Quebec and Montreal* militia, flanking the Far Right, encountered stiff opposition from Townshend's (Howe's) Light Infantry, which had been brought up from the rear to repel snipers.

Meanwhile, Wolfe had ordered the Redcoats to take their posts. And the British soldiers arose to steadfastly hold their places. They waited for the order to fire. This is what they had trained for. Wolfe had literally written the British Army textbook instruction for two platoons firing (dividing a Company into two Platoons, each with its own Captain.) Three discharges per minute with Brown Bess were deliverable in relative ease. Every barrel had been crammed with two or more ammo balls. Some accuracy was possible within seventy-five feet; but these troops fired first from forty feet, with fifty-percent of their projectiles killing.

From clouds of white smoke the British platoons volley fired, one after the other, several times, making a deafening thunder that shattered the French.

"*Vive La France!*

"Long live *King Louie!*"

"Three cheers for the King!"

The battle-cry abruptly died in the pain-racked air. Then without official sanction Frasers Highlanders put down their firearms and wielding broadswords charged upon the disorderly retreating enemy. Other British Regiments followed suite with cold bayonet. But the eleven-minute battle was not without remorse for England. General Wolfe took three shots (wrist, and twice in the torso). The fatal wound occurred at the peak of victory upon *the Plain*.

A romantic interpretation exists that Wolfe fell off his horse in battle, like 'a King Arthur Knight' knocked off his charger with a lance during a tournament dueling joust. In reality, a much different picture has been presented.

Benjamin West (1738-1820) the first American born painter to attain an international reputation, disregarded the advice of King and Parliament, and exhibited his reported Eye-Witnesses historical account: *Death of General Wolfe* (1771) -- [oils on canvas, 1.52 X 2.4 m (~ 3' 3" X 6' 5")]. English Art was never the same, again. Benjamin West portrayed the dying Wolfe and other figures unlike ancient Greeks or Romans, as the traditional rules and customs of History Painting dictated, but rather in eighteenth century clothes, such as those worn on that fateful day of battle September 12, 1759. Major General James Wolfe is shown as a Deposition, Jesus Christ taken down at the foot of the cross after his death.

Mark Cronath was not included in the group at Wolfe's death, but a North American Indian was featured in West's composition, as a foreground figure symbolizing Canada and the New World's continent. The warrior sachem must have been the only representative of the Iroquois present at the battle. Cronath probably begrudgingly tolerated this seated, muscular, and semi-naked savage, whose inclusion in the painting enabled Benjamin West the artist to show an almost complete study of a Nude.

Iroquois controlled the Ohio area and much of the

frontier between Canada and the Thirteen British colo-
nies: Massachusetts, Virginia, New York, Pennsylvania,
New Jersey, Connecticut, New Hampshire, Rhode Island,
Delaware, Maryland, North Carolina, South Carolina,
and Georgia. The Iroquois smoked *the Calumet* or Peace
Pipe to ally with England through the *Covenant Chain* and
Iroquois Confederacy: Mohawk, Seneca, Oneida, Onondaga,
Cayuga, -- and Tuscarora (the Six Nations).

"It's all over for me," said Wolfe, denying the Surgeon. The
General expressed satisfaction that through his heroic sacrifice
Britain had won the day. He was immediately canonized to
Immortal Glory. And his last battle is everywhere considered
one of the ten most important battles in the history of mankind.

Aboard *the Sutherland* the received semaphore relayed:

"Egad! Sir, The enemy runs."

"They can't prevent our taking *the Burgie*," shouted the
Signalman.

Osborn sighed in relief. Breeching high-walled Quebec
City meant conquest of all North America for Britannia. The
great debate over, English will triumph as the first language in
the New World! And he could go back to his Inn and a blithe,
summer tourist trade on the Isle of Wight, in St. George's
Channel between southern England and Ireland.

"*DONNACONAN*," he gleefully exclaimed, "I love your
daughter!"

Seconds later, a solemn *communique* updated the situation:

"The General is dead. Ready the ship to take aboard his
corpse."

Brigadier General Murray had been wounded on horseback. Perhaps the jousting myth was conceived because of that
incident. Monckton also had been wounded. He had been
taken aboard *Lowestoft* (28 gun) frigate. Absolute command

had devolved to Townshend who rode a tall black horse taken from Howe. The Brigadier General arrived, as Wolfe's corpse was being moved off the on the Far Right side of the battle-field. Everything was in disorder. Dead and dying scattered *the Plain* like unnatural mutant growths.

To restore order, Highlanders were summoned with 'Recall', prisoners rounded up, and muskets and other weap-ons gathered. Regiments re-assembled, and trench-works started (that attack from *Bougainville's* army might be met with military efficiency) where the Red Lines fatal to the French had first been drawn. A sergeant and two soldiers shoved a hands-behind-his-back-bound enemy sharpshooter, prisoner of war before the horseman;

"He's confessed to killing the General," the Sergeant reported.

George Townshend, who was actually also a Member of Parliament, looked inquiringly at the killer.

"I seek English mercy," said, the murderer.

"Kneel him down," ordered the Brigadier, "for summarily court-martialed execution: -- guilty!" From high in the saddle Townshend shot the murderer in the back of the head with a hand-gun. He killed him. The body flung forward from the impact of the pistol's punch and the bullet's victim licked the dust. The big black horse pulled to the near side away from the gunblast. And he snorted and threw his noble head, his magnificent mane rippling. One could smell the water of the river in the air.

Major Barry who had been responsible for Howe's com-mandeered horses had had half his face shot off. He and other wounded were attended to. Purple gore a-streaming, men died in affliction, truncated horror and anguish. . . 'They lend the eye a terrible aspect.'

A British sniper's bullet had penetrated *the Marquis's* stomach. Soldiers on each side held him like a Knight in the saddle of *Montparnasse,* his valorous black horse, as crowding ganglike groups rushed him towards the *Saint-Jean Gate. Montcalm* took a quick glance at the battlefield where hundreds of his veterans, Frenchmen, Canadians and their Indian allies inertly lied dead-as-doornails or writhed in wounded torment . Through the hazy purpling he perceived an illusion of *Erebus,* the Greek underworld, where later those slaughtered heroes should rest in pleasant *Elysian Fields* with the shades of great warriors. But for now only the mud, bloodied grass and dirty puddles of rainwater offered up the dead, maimed and mutilated bodies of his comrades in arms. He knew that he, himself, *Louis Joseph the Marquis de Montcalm* was dying for France and that he should never again see his wife or nine children.

In the quiet room lit by only one tall Pascal Candle, the Marquis twisted in atrophy on the bed in a back room of the Ursuline Convent. *General Levis* and *Governor Vaudreuil* stood beside the bed in flickering shadows that he could inform them to continue to fight against a British siege; or they could escape now with the surviving soldiers of the army and unite with *Bougainville,* which they did choose to do. *Bigot* and *Levele* were absent for they had fled to Montreal. *Montcalm* died the next morning under the care of Ursuline Nuns. *Ramezay* surrendered *the City* within a week of *the Marquis de Montcalm's* death

Francis Parkman (1823-1893), Harvard's great historian of France in North America, said that the French estimated their forces at from 3,500 to 7,520 killed or seriously wounded. Brigadier Townshend's account still available in the Public Record Office is: 4,441 English participants.

EPILOGUE

Bosun's Pipes acknowledged the coming aboard of the Union Jack, battle-flag draped, corpse of the General Wolfe, martyred hero at the birth of an Empire. Marines with rifles stood to attention, as a cannonade of twenty-one guns commenced. Simultaneously, Vice Admiral Sir Charles Saunders saluted, and a deck of officers did likewise. The ship took the body below to clean, to embalm and to wrap in a white quilted cotton dressing-gown. They transferred the deceased to the fast sailing sloop, *H.M.S. Royal William,* upon the wine dark sea, to England.

Townshend agreed to the Article of Confederation with *Jean-Baptiste Nicolas Roch de Ramezay:* honours of wars; protection of citizens and property; Roman Catholic Religion allowed; etcetera. British entered *the City* with Flying Colours, pipes and drums. London, when hearing of the victory went ecstatic: bells ringing non-stop, and drinking and dancing in the streets. Townshend hurried back home. Brigadier General Murray became *Governor-General* of Quebec City, and weathered the frozen winter occupation.

Joan Dubois, (Godmother of Karen Bluejeans), under Brigadier General Robert Murray's administration, died in the cold, hunger and disease. She had been diagnosed with what later was called *Tuberculosis*, caused by infection, which had been passed in airborne droplets of coughing and sneezing, to fashion deadly bacteria within her lungs. Her natural immune system could not sustain her bloodstream because her lymph nodes were malfunctioning, due to their excessive strain while she was working as a helper to the Ursuline Nuns tending wounded, sick and dying soldiers (1760). Like all of the others she was stacked until Spring when the ground should have thawed enough to bury the dead.

Meanwhile, the Major General James Wolfe was received with national grief. No more the ringing bells and joyful celebrating. Like Wolfe's mother, Catherine Bolton dressed in black, not unlike a grieving widow. The burial processional took almost two hours to pass before the soldiers, sailors, marines and policemen lined streets that held back the crowds of mourners. The funeral cortege's caisson-transported coffin followed mounted muffled drums, and a mounted flag-bearer of Wolfe's yellow flag (with the black skull in three-quarter profile and the motto): "Death Or Glory!" Wolfe had attained both; and therefore, his body was entombed in Westminster Abbey, the Coronation Hall of Great Britain's Kings & Queens.

In Quebec City, Spring set the stage for Murray to meet *Levis* upon *the Plain of Abraham* for a second battle; but this time the French were attacking *the City* and the British were rushing out to defend it. Like *Montcalm*, Murray was defeated on the field of battle; however the French did not immediately capitalize upon the situation and Quebec remained in British hands. Sick, malnourished and running low on ammunition, the British prepared to engage in house to house fighting if necessary before capitulating. And then, as the St. Lawrence thawed, a pennant of St. George's Cross flapped on the horizon. A British Man-of-War had arrived with fuel, food and other desperately needed supplies. The French fled to re-group at *Montreal*.

In a three pronged attack Major General Amherst, the Commander and Chief of the British forces in the New World, with Brigadier General William Haviland and Brigadier General James Murray captured Canada's capital, *the City of Montreal* (1760), denying military honors; hence, *Levis* and remaining troops burnt their regimental flags. Although there wasn't a major battle, some skirmishing ensued, in which *Jacques-Louis* (the Godfather of Karen Bluejeans) died. He left no son to mourn him. *Jacques-Pierre* had vanished during the Home Guard's sneak attack.

Dominique Francois Louis Du Louches was robbed on his journey to *Montreal*; he died of blunt instrument wounds; but he was left un-scalped, which suggests that Indians probably weren't his assassins. His false hand was missing from his cadaver. Bishop *Levele* returned to Vatican. *Francois Bigot* went on trial in France and was fined and exiled to Switzerland.

Pontiac's War, Pontiac's Rebellion and Pontiac's Conspiracy (1763-66) refer to the same series of events in the *pays d'en haute* or 'upper country' of the Great Lakes region, Illinois Country and the Ohio Country. Britain's *Treaty of 1763* allocated the Ohio Country to the Native Americans; but the Indians in the West felt betrayed. And also since Amherst was against gift giving, an Indian uprising occurred (Ottawa, Ojibwas, Wyandot, Potawatami, Hurons, Miamis, Weas, Kickapoos, Mascoutens, Piankashaws, Delawares, Shawnees, Mingoes and Seneca) against the British, which included Ottawa Chief Pontiac's siege of *Detroit* and other forts in the West. *Neolin*, 'the Delaware Prophet,' preached against trade goods, alcohol and the ways of the white world. Colonel Henry Bouquet offered smallpox- infested blankets to the tribes, as a sort of biological warfare costing up to 1.5 million Native American lives.

Bouquet initiated *The Battle of Bloody Run* to surprise Pontiac but it ended in Indian victory. Mark Cronath died in heroic rear guard action to cover two soldiers who were carrying back a wounded comrade. His body received over twenty-one arrows before he was scalped. Finally, Bouquet in Pennsylvania brought Delaware and Shawnee to sue for peace, which was concluded by Sir William Johnson. Pontiac, "buried the hatchet," and was pardoned with the treaty in 1766. Canada and 'the First Nations' organized policy more like the earlier French fur trade and dramatically reduced tensions. *Golden Bear, Red Feather* and *Rain Cloud* kept to *Above the Falls*. They died in old age as pillars of their community.

But Indians were not the major problem for British authorities. *The Paris Treaty of 1763* along with *The Treaty of Hubertusburg* terminated *the Seven Years War/French & Indian War*. Yet, within twenty years of hostilities ending, the lack of a threat from French-Canadian Indian raids encouraged the Thirteen American Colonies to resent the presence of British troops. The Stamp Act, the Tea Act and other prohibitive legislation by Parliament, amounting to 'Taxation without Representation' caused the Sons of Liberty and other Yankee Doodle/Liberty Bell/ Stars-&-Stripes rebels to protest. Thomas Jefferson drafted *The Declaration of Independence* in 1776; and battles between British troops and American Minutemen & Continentals ensued: Lexington, Concord, Bunker Hill, Trenton, Saratoga and others until the band played *the World Turned Upside Down*, and Britain's Lord Cornwallis surrendered to George Washington at Yorktown. The Constitution was ratified; the United States of America became an independent country with George Washington as President, 1789.

That same year, commenced the French Revolution. Notwithstanding Great Britain's generosity towards *Quebecers* in Canada and America's pledge of true friendship to France, the French 'Ship of State' started to sink. The *Ancien Regime's Estates General* – the legislative assembly before the Revolution (Nobles, Clergy and Third Estate *Bourgeoisie*) reformed into a kind of *National Assembly*.

France held Europe's largest population, and a scarcity of food existed. Many influential thinkers and men of action had participated in the American War for Independence, which along with the earlier French & Indian War, had bankrupted France's finances on a *De Facto* basis.

At the *Jeu de Paume*, in June, the 'Tennis Court Oath' not to break up or go rogue until France had a new Constitution was sworn. A Tricolour Cockade (blue, white & red) symbolized *'the Declaration of the Rights of Man and of the Citizen'* in August, which sought social change based on enlightenment to replace the Great Fear (*Grande Peur*) of July, when talk of a conspiracy of the aristocracy and King to overthrow the Third Estate had led to Parisians storming *the Bastille*, the bastion of Royal Absolutism and Dictatorship. The rabble's revolt then had become *the French Revolution* of 1789.

Headed by *Robespierre a* "Reign of Terror," in which tens of thousands lost their lives, the guillotine executed almost 17,000 persons including *King Louis XVI* and Queen Marie *Antoinette.* Upon this stage, *the Corsican, Napoleon Bonaparte* entered history.

In defense of the Convention in the *Tuileries,* 'the little corporal' fired cannon upon the unruly mob, "a whiff of grapeshot," that killed 1,400 royalists. *The Directory* gave him command of the Army; he became *First Consul for Life*; and then he was elected as *"Emperor of the French."* To the tune of *La Marseillaise,* France's *National Anthem, Napoleon* spread Revolutionary fervor and democratic thought (*liberte, egalite, fraternite*) throughout Europe unto the far reaches of Egypt and Russia. At Waterloo, the British Duke of Wellington defeated, *"the Man of Destiny,"* who died in exile on the island of St. Helena in the Atlantic Ocean off the Southwest coast of Africa.

Nevertheless, in 1803, *Napoleon* sold *Louisiana* (828,000 square miles) to the United States under the administration of Thomas Jefferson (*the Louisiana Purchase*) for about $15,000,000. The size of the country was doubled, and most of the land that had not been lost by France during the French & Indian War was transferred to America (Arkansas, Missouri, Iowa, Oklahoma, Kansas, Nebraska, Minnesota, North Dakota, South Dakota, New Mexico, a portion of Texas, Montana, Wyoming, Colorado and New Orleans). French influence continued: through the names of the states, Maine, Delaware, Louisiana and others; and, the appellation of many cities such as New Orleans, Des Moines and Baton Rouge, and the introduction of French words into the English language like caribou, cuisine and toboggan. .

The triumph of the English Language, its adaptation into Standard American English (SAE), and also the importance of English as a Second Language (ESL) because of Wolfe's victory at Quebec City, earned emphasis in the conclusion of Philip Parkerman's book, *Legend of Karen Bluejeans,* which became a national bestseller, as well as a great international commercial success. Rakel, his sponsor, received recognition as, *"a light unto the nations!"*

And Rakel Cohen married Philip Parkerman. They have

a traditional Jewish wedding, with: *Chuppah, Huppah* or *Hoopla –Wedding Canopy,* (an ornamental silk sheet stretched over four poles to symbolize the house of the wedding couple); the signing of the wedding contract and exchange of wedding rings; seven blessings; breaking of a wine glass (to remember Jerusalem and the destruction of the Temple). Rakel's fingers were temporarily tattooed (in red-earth colored or henna-dyed ink) with ancient mystical Judaic markings from the *Kabala.*

Prior to the marriage ceremony, she wore golden bangles across the forehead of her veil. There had been discussion over what should be uttered as her veil was removed. The bride's mother Sarah Israel wanted the traditional blessing given in *Genesis* to Rebekah:

"Our sister, be thou the mother of thousands of ten thousands, and let thy seed possess the gate of those that hate them."

Ben Cohen, the bride's father agreed with his wife but insisted that instead of, "be thou," a closer translation of the Hebrew utterance, that is quite simply: "become." Rakel approved more of her father's preference not only because his seemed to be more existential ('the coming into being aspect' of it); but also because "become" was closer to the early Hebrew, whose use was important for the realization of *Zionism,* modern Jewry and *the State of Israel*:

"Our sister, become the mother of thousands of ten thousands, and let thy seed possess the gate of those that hate them."

Mendelsohn's *Wedding March* from *Midsummer Night's Dream* was played.

While at the Hilton Hotel on their Honeymoon, the newlyweds viewed a foreign Press Conference *via* satellite from Vienna. A Baron had uncovered an old oil painting in his castle's cellar. Portrait of the legendary Karen Bluejeans? The Maple tree visible in the picture's background enriched the interest of Japanese buyers of Art.

A French reporter asks the Baron if the family's fortune had been enlarged by the treasures of Jews in Nazi concentration camps during WWII. With her lilting French accent, the stylish, blond Countess translates his reply: " 'No Jews are involved', he says, 'Karen Bluejeans makes her stand at the Pass. She is wearing the Redcoat of a British Officer's Uniform. Look! She stands on guard for thee!"